The Light of Winter

FIRST EDITION

ISBNs:
978-1-80227-910-8 (eBook)
978-1-80227-911-5 (Paperback)
978-1-80541-003-4 (Hardback)

THE LIGHT OF WINTER

TROIAN W ANDERSON

This book is dedicated to our Late Majesty Queen Elizabeth II
and women the world over.

Honesty, Integrity, Love and Faith.
These were the pillars of her life.
The love of nations.
The ability to make one comfortable in her presence
and see others as equals.
All carried out with great humility.

Only now do we learn the extent of her kindness, compassion, wit,
and the exemplary life lived.
It would appear we love her more
in death than we did in life.

And therein lies the lesson.

Learn about people, rather than believe our
personal and suggested misguided assumptions.

A JOYOUS WAY TO LIVE.
If you so choose.

FOR MY GIRLS
Lynne the Mother, Amanda the Patient, Sarah the Wise,
Rachel the Nurturer, Charlotte the Resilient, Caitlin the Younger
and Zoe the Potential.

AND MY IMPRESSIONABLE GIRLS
Grace the Lady, Ffion the Witty, Sienna the Weirdo,
Millie the Quiet and Harper the Joy.

Acknowledgements

I suppose it began many years ago with a visit to a fortune teller.

Excited to learn of what could be, I listened intently. Toward the end of my reading I was told I would die before a certain age.

Being a firm believer in the afterlife and such, I took this on board but with a pinch of salt, because time is subjective, and this was so far into the future there was no need to worry about it yet . As the years went by and this particular birthday grew closer, I would think of this prediction on a more regular basis, but not so much so that it affected my daily life.

Though I loved my work, it did occasionally become the daily grind (at that time I was a chef), however, it was that career that gave me the opportunity to travel and eventually migrate.

After my migration I had a complete reversal of lifestyle.

I really was living my dream and eight years in the making, I had my moment of Great Revelation, an Epiphany if you will.

The night before the predicted birthday and not wanting to go to sleep that night, I sat in the garden while the others slept.

My mind whirring, conjuring many scenarios of what would happen should the dreaded prediction come to pass.

Almost crying and beginning to shake, and only two cigarettes left from the pack of twenty five, Midnight grew closer.

If this prophecy came to pass, I only had minutes left.

Midnight struck!

DEAD! But still alive.

PHEEEW. Relief.

It wasn't death in the way one would assume, but the death of a mindset and an identity.

Some of the things we hear or are told, if they do come to fruition, rarely will it be how we envision it, so wait for the event and enjoy the experience. The old saying comes to mind;
To Assume makes an **ASS** of **U** and **ME**.

The lifestyle change, as a consequence of my migration caused a very very gradual alteration of my thought processes, and this event brought the clarity I so desperately desired.
I now saw the world in a far clearer light.
So the prophecy did come to pass and it was the old me, my old identity that died.
I wasn't going to let this opportunity pass.
To build an identity **without** inherited beliefs but well researched ones, I knew would bring great peace to me.

I have always loved meeting people and learning of their lives, including struggles, Joys and achievements etc, but in this new land there were nations from all over the world.

There were people from all nations and some from lands where apartheid was law.

When they migrated they brought their mindset with them, and after learning of their lives and life experiences, I understood why they thought the way they did.

On one occasion whilst discussing views and opinions of other races, it was pointed out to them that friends of theirs were of said races.

Their reply was

"But they're different."

What a revelation that was for me.

It showed, regardless of our assumptions and beliefs, if we take the time to get out of our comfort zone and question what we believe to be, more often than not we will prove our assumptions and beliefs incorrect.

(Maybe that's why we are never taught to question them. We always want to be right, and the person we know always tells us the truth is us! Even when cognitive dissonance sets in, we always know the truth.)

Arewe really our identity?

It's the people of the world that make it the beautiful enchanting place it has always been, so travel, engage, and with an open mind, one by one, eliminate your prejudices.

I took my own advice and met many wonderful people along the the way, many became friends and many became the family I chose for myself.

So for the family I have and the family I chose:–
Amanda.
You have been so patient, understanding, encouraging and helpful in creating my vision, and I'm sorry to inform you but this is the tip of the iceberg. Without your support this would not be.

Sarah.
For the gift that inspired this story, all you've done to help this see the light of day and just for being you.

Naomi Fitzgerald.
My Anchor, guinea pig, sounding board and guide, you have been instrumental in all of this and more, for which I will be eternally grateful.

Graham "Picasso" Griffiths.
For your advice, direction and support during this and other projects, your friendship of so many years, your off the wall crazy fantastic ideas and artwork.

Dr Stuart Elsworthy for your deep friendship, the encouragement and advice during this and other projects.

Tess Maria for our lifelong friendship, varied conversations including the suggestion of a pseudonym. Very wise of you.

And for friends and contributors:–

Gary Jones for your kindness and support, and for giving me the time to complete this project.

Stephen Jenkins especially and my first term classmates at Creative Writing, Garth Olwg, Mary-Lou, Rebecca, Paul, Adrian, Elaine, for all insights shared and especially Sarah for introducing me to VANTABLACK.

Credits:
To Publishing Push and all staff included in this project, Sophie, Ben, especially Amy, for her meticulous work to make this what it has become, and Gladys for her care, interest, professionalism, and friendliness. Noel, for formatting the book. Thank you!

If we don't know, we assume.
Most of life is an assumption.

Don't live an assumed life,
MAKE KNOWN THE UNKNOWN!

It was time.

The last supernova visible from Earth was in 1054 and it lasted twenty-three days, but this was very different.

A jar in Earth's rotation caused a ripple throughout the galaxy, awakening long dormant energies. The universal equilibrium, momentarily off kilter, released something that was to bring great change to humanity. Its current direction of travel as a species was heading back to the Stone Age.

NASA

One of the primary mirror panels now had six indentations. With eighteen mirrors in total, NASA were hopeful the damage wouldn't impact their search beyond the Big Bang.

With infinite space available to them, they chanced on a small area at the time of the coming of the seven.

The new James Webb telescope captured the light anomaly immediately before partial destruction. It appeared to be a supernova, but excitement and devastation experienced simultaneously left the NASA scientists dumbstruck and panicked. The debris impacted with such force a complete blackout ensued and the coming weeks were focused, stressful and full of anticipation.

Excitement built over the period of recalibration and the night finally arrived. With the scientists poised at their computers, anxious to enter coordinates, the ambience was electric, but silent.

The numbers were entered and while the telescope tracked towards its pre-determined position, they sat engrossed in their monitors, waiting for images to be streamed.

They couldn't believe their eyes. All present were baffled.

There were no remnants of the supernova.

Staring at the empty space, the black hole and neutron star were conspicuous by their absence. They had no evidence to verify the only image of this anomaly.

Was this a chance impact or universal forces keeping harmony?

Though reported without the required evidence, the official line taken by NASA was this.

With only a solitary image, the suspected supernova witnessed by the James Webb telescope was an error in analysis. Rays from the sun reflecting from the back of the moon during the solar eclipse onto what they believed to be distant space debris displayed itself as a carbon copy of supernova properties.

This caused astronomical refraction of light on a scale never before witnessed from debris and this was the basis of the agency's error.

Their embarrassment was felt worldwide.

Antonis

As a youngster, Antonis was an aspiring actor with a very bright future. His research and imagination were so comprehensive, he knew his characters inside out. He played them so convincingly he could have been each and every one he portrayed.

This was cut short after the sudden loss of a loved one caused him to re-evaluate his life. This was when he discovered philosophy. He was so taken with this school of thought, everything he believed important to his life fell by the wayside, and as he sat, quietly contemplating in his government office, he felt the ripple.

He knew this was the beginning of the end and would result in his long-awaited omnipotence.

Lifetimes within a life, his searching produced his first real result by chance, and his knowledge of other worlds spurred him to re-evaluate his government position and find a job that would assist him in finally ending his search.

Joseph

Surprising for such a young man, but it was no coincidence that his drinks of choice were stouts and porters.

Engraved with his name and a weather map, he held his favourite pint glass with an unsteady hand. Crystal clear with facets spiralling top to bottom, he slowly poured his new find.

The vision and aroma began to settle him.

As a lover of coffee and of stout, this was his perfect blend.

Once the dark fluid velvet escaped the bottle, its aroma filled the room, changing the ambience from a quiet, lonely and oppressive kitchen to that of a vibrant coffee house and, through his anguish, it immediately teased a smile.

From the bending of the cap releasing the gas to the final sip, this wasn't a drink to be glugged. It was a delight for all the senses.

He wasn't a drinker, but an appreciator of quality. As a consequence, six beers in, he was almost asleep, but still contemplating what interim position he could apply for whilst considering his future.

Tired in his stupor, he studied the bottle's label. With such a flavourful character, he was affronted by the emblazoned "Coffee Stout".

Without a doubt, this should be a porter, he thought. Between contemplations of interim jobs and beer classifications, he concluded, *Yes, definitely a porter.*

As he drifted off to sleep, he was wondering hotel, train station or hospital.

Antonis

The nameplate on the office door read:

BACKLAV. A.
Director of Science

Antonis was always known, and only every referred to, as Ant. He insisted on the unusual placing of his initial after his surname. Being read that way conjured deceptive perceptions, especially for foodies and others who knew of the dessert.

A former government minister, everyone knew of his appointment weeks before commencement, causing speculation as to what kind of person he was and the type of boss he would be. To most, his name suggested a sweet man of many layers with something hidden within.

Amongst the staff, there were those with a tendency towards the spiritual and though he looked mid-forties, they described him as an old soul, saying he'd been here before, meaning they believed him to have been incarnated many times.

This was not the case.

Though his handbag intrigued some, his introduction to the senior staff went very well.

He had an uncanny ability of reading people and, with a great understanding of body language and interpretation of facial expressions, without exception, all were an open book to him.

He pandered to what he knew each individual expected of this first meeting and portrayed himself accordingly.

The staff believed at least two of their guesses were correct, but only time would tell if there really was something hidden deep within.

During the first month as he settled in, he made a point of making himself known to every member of staff including personal meetings with those that were to report to him directly. This was when the gossip of his insistence on punctuality began.

Joseph

Joseph was one of the last members of staff Ant met with. A focused intelligent young man who never suffered fools gladly.

Punctuality was important to him too. He made his way to Mr Backlav's office and he was on schedule to arrive at the office slightly earlier than necessary.

His colleague Andrew caught sight of him as he passed.

"Joseph," he shouted.

He stopped and walked back to the glass-fronted office.

"Do you have the forecast models for the next two months? The meeting was brought forward and I have to give a presentation to the directors first thing tomorrow morning and I'm way behind schedule."

The visual prediction software on the recently installed state-of-the-art computer system was underperforming; its accuracy trending far below the promise of the supplier and expectations of the directors and government ministers.

"That meeting isn't due until the end of the week," Joseph replied.

"I know. They sprung it on me twenty minutes ago and I'll have to work late tonight to be ready by the morning."

"It's almost complete. I can get it to you after my meeting."

Andrew continued the conversation. "Who's your meeting with?"

"Mr Backlav," he replied as he looked at his watch. "Shit!"

It was just approaching four fifteen.

"I have to go. I'll get them to you as soon as I get back."

Rushing along the corridor, he decided against the lift and taking three steps at a time, he arrived on the fourth floor out of breath. With a quick pace, he read the nameplates as he passed.

UMA N. SEAN

Chief People Officer

COLIN LEER

Programmes Director

C. C. SEYMOUR

Technology Director/Chief Information Officer

OMAR BILAL SERVIR

Services Director

Arriving at the office door at the end of the hall, he noticed the unusual placement of the initial and made a mental note to ask the director at the end of his meeting.

"Knock, knock."

"Come in, Joseph."

Before he could apologise and explain his lateness, Antonis said, "You're late."

Joseph began to explain but was cut short by Antonis raising his index finger to subtly pursed lips.

"Punctuality and order. Some of the keys to success."

A strange statement, Joseph thought, but as he quickly scanned the room, he noticed an order to it. On entering, he knew this was the director's space. Almost feng shui, but not.

The energy was off.

Assisting the flow of energy throughout, all elements were represented. There was an excessive amount of metal in the form of shelving units, abstract sculptures and unexpected water features. They were specifically placed, but were of a forced water design, fountain-like and not the free-flowing nature of a waterfall.

His eyes finally rested on the curious sight on Ant's desk.

The marble and the bag.

Though Joseph knew he had been late, it was only by two minutes.

Antonis remained calm and said, "Friday at quarter past four. See you then."

Joseph stood speechless. He had plans for his half day Friday, but he dared not attempt rearranging and, comprehending the mood of the room, he offered no reply.

Without a word, he turned and headed for the door.

Reaching for the handle, he noticed Ant's mission statement.

Taking pride of place on the back of the office door hung a hand carved, thin stone tablet within an ivory and gold inlay frame. It looked like an ancient artefact with one word only: ACHIEVE.

All that entered read it on exit, and it was always in Ant's view.

From behind him, he heard Ant say, "Do it!"

Joseph left and closed the door behind him.

There was something not quite right about the director, and he had Ant's cards marked from the start.

Paying more attention as he made his way back to his desk, the synchronicity of the nameplates stirred something within.

He remembered the day Ant was introduced.

The CEO and only these four of the many directors and officers were present. He wondered if there was any significance to this and his appointment.

Antonis

All meetings were scheduled for fifteen minutes past four in the afternoon.

Numbers were as important to him as precision and accuracy. He understood timing was everything to achieve the results he desired.

Staff weren't invited in until thirty seconds before their appointment. This was just enough time for them to enter the room and take a seat.

This gave Ant the three minutes he required to inform each person of his expectations from their one-to-one. Whether they were sat or not, he would begin at precisely quarter past. Sat with his arm slightly raised in front of him, he stared at his rose gold and grey LIV GX-Diver's watch. He wasn't a diver and it wasn't the most expensive watch, but by far it was one of the most accurate timepieces on the market.

During every introductory meeting, he would stop talking three seconds before the eighteenth minute to allow the other person to begin at four eighteen precisely.

This was crucial.

The meetings were formatted in a way that allowed the person to feel comfortable in his presence. He was a captivating man when necessary and, without exception, each staff member, trance-like and without prompt, would disclose many things about their lives; some things quite unnecessarily.

Those on time enjoyed their meeting and thought of him as very friendly but they couldn't have been more wrong.

After their meetings, Ant knew the members of staff discussed between themselves their perceptions of him.

They all liked him but the consistent curiosity surrounding the precisely placed marble and bag, and the order of his office, overtook the basis of conversation.

Knowing people have their individual quirks, like strange items used as lucky charms or doing things in a specific order to achieve a desired outcome, they accepted this as an eccentricity of his. The marble was odd though.

The coloured glass within was not what any of them expected to see. The form of an ear took the place of the usual wavy strands of encased colour. The bag, a tan coloured Radley, was odd too. Not because of the gold-coloured Scottie dog bag charm or the occasional wave-like shimmer, but just because it was there.

A woman's handbag

Formerly the Minister for Science, he resigned his post as it was no longer tenable due to the Prime Minister's incompetence, or so he said. In reality, it was no longer tenable because the results he required personally were not being achieved, and there was no way he could use his powers to achieve them as this would expose him and possibly his lifelong quest.

A master of connections, he permeated all realities, and the information he possessed prior to this point had been gathered over millennia, but the recently acquired information from his widely dispersed, multi-dimensional and genetically imbued drones was all pointing to a weather event.

To give up was never a consideration. The prize was too great.

Resigning his ministerial post was necessary as past intel gathering had been fruitless and now it had become a weather-related goal. Now was the perfect time for him to become involved with the Meteorological Service of Canada.

He was the only candidate they wanted and their devious ways made that happen.

Once appointed, making headway was now certain.

—o—

With the installation of the new software complete, data from previous years was entered. The meteorological team's first task was to determine if the software could in fact predict weather patterns, their course and intensity almost two years in advance.

Many were sceptical of the new technology, especially the older staff who scoffed at the cost along with the impossibility. The younger generation were far more receptive and diligent in their attempted mastery of the software, but on completion of transferring twenty years worth of data, the software struggled to attain an accuracy over sixty percent. Although above average and far higher than some expected, it didn't warrant the cost.

Comfortable with their knowledge of the old system, the older staff continued with what they knew, always comparing results to prove their point. As months went by, the accuracy induced arrogance, so it wasn't "out of the blue" as they insisted. Antonis' staff should have taken the information on board instead of dismissing it as an impossibility. After all, they'd been relentless in their attempts for accuracy since the installation of the visual prediction software. Yet, they were having great difficulty in accepting the reality of the information that had been consistently given to them for almost a month now.

It was more disbelief than surprise, and only now was the certainty of it all finally beginning to sink in. The impending severity of the storm was far worse than anyone thought possible as nothing of this scale has been witnessed in recorded history. The Meteorological Service of Canada had to get this one right.

They still had time.

What started as a long-range forecast was rapidly approaching, and due to their arrogance, they foolishly insisted on trying to obtain drastically different results with a majority of the same data. Many different scenarios were entered into the programme, but without fail, the end results had only minor and insignificant differences. As a consequence, predictions, coupled with the fact the accuracy of their state-of-the-art system wasn't what they believed it should be, always left an element of doubt in their minds and when they eventually succumbed to the reality of what Canada was facing, there was an urgency to have this information distributed to government and relevant agencies.

As part of their report, they could not overestimate how bad it was going to be and, after consulting with the government, directives were given on what recommended precautions and procedures should be taken prior to the event to ensure everyone's safety.

Joseph

The vacuum of the storm held the doors slightly ajar.

Unable to stop himself, Joseph stood there peering through the gap.

No one saw.

Curious as to what held their focus, he too looked up.

With no ceiling to the room or roof to the building, he could see clear sky encircled by dense black cloud. The rumbling of thunder grew louder by the second eventually releasing a charge of energy so big, the building shook.

It carved a path through the top of the building, over the patient, snake-like through the staff, terminating at his feet. The power of the bolt threw him to the end of the corridor, smashing past chairs and trolleys to land unconscious next to the water cooler.

Morty and Ellen

On one hand, Ellen was thankful her baby wasn't due for another two months. If she went into labour during the storm, the logistics of getting to hospital would be unpredictable, but another two months carrying around what felt and looked like triplets was a dreadful thought. Only just entering the third trimester, her belly was unusually large for a first pregnancy.

Yesterday was strangely odd, considering what the whole country had in store. For the past week, all weather channels were reporting on Storm Crystal and why it would be the worst in recorded history. The meteorologists were so convinced of its impending furore that it became the main news story for the week leading up to its landfall.

The Meteorological Service of Canada was, surprisingly, precise on the timing, not that it affected Morty and Ellen any differently than other members of the public, but for all the scenarios that were input, far-reaching events lay ahead for everyone.

—o—

Morty and Ellen arrived at the hospital after calling an ambulance due to some minor blood loss.

The previous afternoon, Ellen was rearranging the furniture in the lounge; not that it was going to be that different, but she loved change, no matter how subtle. She wanted the TV slightly offset from the large arched window that overlooked the garden so whenever she was on the sofa, whether the TV was on or not, her gaze would catch the variety of wildlife that visited their garden. The sofa and armchairs easily slid over the carpet as she dragged them. However, the TV was slightly heavier and more awkward than she had expected, though she did manage to lift it off the stand and gently place it on the floor.

She dragged the TV unit and positioned it off-centre beneath the window then proceeded to lift and carry the TV to its new location. The lift gave her a slight twinge in her tummy and she quickly caught her breath, but she thought nothing of it and continued with the rest of the room, singing quietly to herself.

After a somewhat strenuous day, she sat with her herbal-infused tonic and relaxed for a while. As dusk drew closer, she felt the need for an early night. Morty stayed up a little later, so Ellen could get to sleep before he started snoring.

At precisely 11:11 p.m., Ellen was awoken by a wet sensation slowly moving across her inner thigh. She quietly got out of bed and went to the bathroom. Initially, she thought it may have been her waters breaking. But being too early in the pregnancy for that to happen, it wasn't the gush she expected it to be.

When she put the bathroom light on, she was horrified to see a thick, moist and partly crusty scarlet ribbon seeping towards her knee. It wasn't much but it was enough to have woken her and, being her first pregnancy, she was slightly panicked and unsure what this meant for her baby.

Feeling herself beginning to well up, she rushed back to the bedroom and woke her husband.

"Morty, Morty, wake up," she whispered.

Bleary eyed and slightly startled, he said, "What's wrong?"

As she was telling him, he told her to lie on the bed, then scanned the room for his mobile phone.

It wasn't in its usual place. Neither of their mobile phones were in the bedroom.

Not wanting to waste time looking, he hurried downstairs to the house phone. He dialled the emergency services and explained their situation.

An ambulance was dispatched immediately with an estimated time of arrival of 11:50.

Morty packed some necessities for Ellen and waited for the ambulance to arrive.

After only ten minutes, there was a knock at the door. He rushed downstairs, let the paramedics in and, as they followed him to the bedroom, he hastily explained what had happened.

Telling him to slow down and repeat, they entered the room to find Ellen sobbing on the bed.

The paramedics calmed them and checked her over and due to how distraught she was, they decided it would be safest for the baby if Ellen was admitted to hospital, if only just to monitor her.

They arrived and were taken to the maternity ward where Carla, the duty midwife, came over and had a chat with them both.

"I don't think this is anything for you to worry about. I know it's no consolation, but minor blood loss at this stage of pregnancy is rarely serious and far more common than most people think. So, try to relax. But we do need a urine sample," she said as she gave Ellen a sterile container. "Once you're done, I'll be back to give you a thorough check up."

Ellen obliged and, on her return, Carla pulled the curtains around the bed and proceeded with her examination. With an ear trumpet on Ellen's stomach, she listened intently to locate the baby's heartbeat, then began palpating to determine the baby's position. Apart from the size, everything appeared to be normal, so she continued to check if Ellen had started to dilate.

On completion of the assessment, sensors were placed on Ellen's tummy for monitoring whilst Carla questioned the accuracy of her dates.

Once bloods had been taken and her blood pressure was deemed okay, Carla said, "Baby feels larger than normal for seven months, so I'm going to arrange an ultrasound to confirm your due date is correct and ensure there's no placental abruption."

Not understanding the seriousness of the potential placenta issue, they were relieved by the results and Carla's calming manner. With it still being very early in the morning and a while before the ultrasound, they relaxed.

Ellen fell asleep almost immediately, but it took Morty a little longer as the comfort of the chair left a lot to be desired.

Comfortable in the belief that everything was fine, they were looking forward to going home later that day. Not giving a second thought to the impending storm.

Joseph

Forecasting this far in advance was still an experimental procedure for them. With almost two years of data already analysed, most of the senior staff were now tracking the storm, monitoring any minor changes in real time and no longer considering previous and current forecasts.

A diligent and dedicated young man, Joseph was eager to make his mark as a junior meteorologist. He'd been working on a variety of forecast models prior to the formation of Storm Crystal and, never having the need for much sleep, he was always first to work and, most of the time, one of the last to leave.

He was currently working on the seventh forecast because the previous three grew gradually more sinister. His method of working was to create forecasts for personal surety and in all previous cases, four was enough. His analysis of the first two forecasts showed nothing unexpected, so the last forecast would be his personal confirmation of the previous, but this one developed an anomaly.

Once the eye of the storm had formed, it appeared to expel three smaller eyes which began to encircle the central eye.

Thinking he had inadvertently entered incorrect data, he proceeded with forecast four. This emulated the third and his diligence, along with OCD, spurred him to continue.

Forecast five did the same as number four throwing out another three storm centres. The only differences in his data entry were the meteorological variables, wind, pressure and temperature.

Though the devastation of the storm would see hundreds of thousands of people displaced with catastrophic consequences, the onscreen visual display was beautifully mesmerising; six lesser storm centres gently pulsating in size and colour, circling the main.

He realised the urgency of his findings should they come to pass and eventually pulled himself from his self-induced trance and, with feverish haste, sent his results to the science director.

After studying the forecast model, Joseph was called to the director's office.

"You do understand we are approaching a potential national disaster?"

"Yes, sir."

"Then explain this."

As Antonis pressed the button on his remote control, the whole of the wall behind him lit up with Joseph's forecast model.

Initially unsure of what he meant, Joseph couldn't believe the director of science was unable to comprehend his work.

"It's my latest forecast model of the storm, sir."

"Well, I'm sorry to say, but that's ridiculous. Do you know the extremes all variables would have to reach for this forecast to actually happen? Including the atmospheric dynamics and thermodynamics?"

Still confident in his work, albeit a little nervous, Joseph explained in detail the data inputted to achieve the display in front of him and though a plausible explanation, the director was not yet convinced.

"I've been around for far longer than people would believe and I have witnessed every kind of storm. Conceivable and inconceivable. And this falls far beyond the latter!"

He gave Joseph some statistical advice to consider and suggested he re-examine his work.

Despondent, Joseph left the office, wondering how the stats suggested could impact his work in any way.

Remembering the solitary word from the tablet on the director's door, he sat at his desk and reluctantly amended a small portion of his data with the information given.

On completion, he pressed play.

During the first twenty-five seconds of a thirty-second clip, his conceitedness grew incrementally.

I knew I was right! I have to find a way to convince him this will be the outcome, he thought.

The last five seconds played out and, with no indication, the six smaller storm centres disappeared.

So confident in his work was he, this was a visual he could not accept. He ran it again and again, but it remained.

Still adamant in the accuracy of his work, yet nothing to back it up, he reluctantly downloaded the visual onto a thumb drive. Not wanting to forward it by email, he took it to the director personally, hoping for an opportunity to attempt an explanation of what he was still trying to figure out himself. Time dragged on his dreaded journey to the director's office. He was tense as he played out various scenarios in his mind of what he would say to convince him.

Standing at the door, he nervously knocked.

After receiving the welcome he expected, he convinced the director to at least look at his findings as he handed over the USB.

Inserted and ready, Antonis pressed play.

Once displayed on the screen wall at the back of the office, Joseph could see the beginnings of an "I told you so" look appear on the director's face.

The defeated feeling was beginning to rise within him. He knew he had to make some attempt at saving the reputation he had created and worked so hard for thus far.

"Sir, though you were obviously correct with the statistical data, I can't help but feel that is not the end of it. Yes, the smaller storm centres no longer appear to be a threat but I don't believe they are gone completely."

"Really? And why's that?"

"Well, on the face of it, the storm evolves as we would expect it to, but I believe the smaller storm centres are still active."

"How can you conclude that? Look at the screen! There is no evidence to substantiate."

"I realise that, but if you look at the stats, the atmospheric pressure is off the charts and the wind speed is increasing at a phenomenal rate."

"Okay, but that still doesn't explain why you think the smaller ones are still present."

"Well, although we have never encountered this before, what I believe is happening here is the atmospheric pressure is compressing the storm making the centre smaller and eliminating from view the surrounding six, simultaneously concentrating and increasing the internal power of it."

"That's quite a prediction. Don't misunderstand my stance on this. I'm not saying it would never happen, but the odds are so astronomical, I think it would be foolish to continue. We have to manage this in real time when it comes to pass. With factual satellite data as we receive it. So, if that's all, I need to get on."

Feeling defeated once again, Joseph reluctantly left the office, noticing the mission statement again. Spurred on by the director's refusal to accept his calculated and educated opinion, he returned to his desk to complete yet another.

Morty and Ellen

The storm had been well under way for over six hours and was now becoming localised. Though it was still over five miles from New Westminster's Royal Colombian Hospital, camera crews were there waiting. The prediction was it would peak in the vicinity of the hospital.

All news channels were giving it intense coverage.

It was just after 2 p.m. and the hospital porter had arrived at Ellen's bed to take her for the scheduled ultrasound. It was almost the end of Carla's shift, but before leaving, she went to reassure Ellen everything would be fine.

Morty helped Ellen into the wheelchair then followed the porter to radiology.

On arrival, the radiologist, Joshua, introduced himself.

"If you pop yourself up onto the bed, get comfortable and lift your gown, we can get started," he instructed.

Once she was comfortable on the bed with the blanket over her bottom half, Ellen raised her gown ready for Joshua to begin.

He proceeded with lubricating fluid on her stomach and began to search for points of the baby from where he would take his measurements. Whilst looking at the screen, he made a number of clicks.

Remembering what he read in Ellen's notes, he was confused by the results, so repeated his measurements again to confirm they were correct.

He mumbled to himself.

"Is everything all right?" Morty asked with some concern.

Ellen looked at Morty as if to ask what was wrong.

"Oh, I'm sorry. I didn't mean to alarm you. It's just that your notes state your due date is March 16, but with the measurements I've just taken, it appears you are already overdue by eighteen days."

Whilst looking at each other in disbelief after Joshua's statement, without warning, there was an almighty WHOOSH.

Ellen's waters broke with intense pressure and she was soaked right the way down to her feet. The bed linen was sodden and dripping to the floor at the lower end of the bed.

That immediately took their minds off what Joshua had just told them.

"Whoa!" Joshua blurted as he jumped back to avoid getting wet. "Okay, don't panic. I'll get some towels to clean you up, and we'll get the porter to take you back to your ward where the midwife can check if you are dilated at all."

When Joshua came back into the room, he helped Morty clean up the mess. Once Ellen was tidied up and ready to go, Joshua called the porter. Fortunately, he'd waited outside the ultrasound suite.

He took Ellen back to the ward with Joshua following behind.

With a short silent escape of gas, Ellen felt like she had a bad case of trapped wind as she manoeuvred herself onto the bed, but apart from that, there was no pain at all.

"Joshua," Ellen said, "How can the dates be so far out? When I had my first scan at twelve weeks to confirm my due date, I was told everything was fine and as they expected it to be."

"Honestly, I have no idea," he said, "I will have to look into it, but if your twelve-week scan was correct, which I'm sure it was, then the only explanation is the baby. Your child appears to have almost doubled its development rate since the first trimester.

"There is no precedent for this. I've double checked my measurements to be sure and they were correct. Therefore, you are overdue and your waters breaking only confirms this."

His statement confused them more and while contemplating this information, another midwife arrived to carry out her internal exam.

The storm was making speedy progress towards the hospital, but in their attempt to comprehend the confusion surrounding Ellen's results, it was of little importance.

Except for the eavesdropping porter. His shift was due to end at five o'clock and he was beginning to get impatient as he didn't want anything to do with a birth on the way to the delivery suite. That would only extend his shift and he wanted to get home before the storm reached its peak.

Ellen's contractions started slowly as the midwife was preparing for the examination. During the process, her contractions were short but intense and on her way to the delivery suite, they increased in frequency and pain. They were now coming thick and fast.

It took seven minutes to get there.

They finally arrived at the delivery suite on the top floor and by the time Ellen was on the bed, prepared and in the stirrups, it was almost four o'clock. When the midwife checked how far along she was, she found almost full dilation so an epidural was pointless. Things were moving extremely quickly and it wouldn't have relieved any pain she was currently suffering.

Ellen felt everything.

Due to the results of her ultrasound, the new duty midwife asked the nurse to request an obstetrician be present.

It was now 16:08.

They couldn't see outside, but the wind and rain had been battering the opaque windows of the delivery suite for some time now, but almost oblivious to this, they continued with the birthing process.

At 16:09, Ellen's contractions stopped. The bad weather seemed to have dissipated and there was a deadly silence. They all stopped what they were doing and looked at each other.

The silence was deafening, not a breath could be heard.

Then, a gentle extraction of air began.

The ventilation system began with a slow quiet rattle, becoming increasingly louder. The invisible force behind the air removal caused the slow inwards movement of the doors. The room vibrated as the negative pressure and sound became almost intolerable. The speed at which the air was now being sucked out of the room violently tore the roof from the building.

All television channels had cameras set up throughout British Columbia, capturing the ferocity of the storm as it made its way through the province, but it was a freelance cameraman at the hospital that captured the storm tearing off the roof.

The delivery suite was in the direct path of the storm's eye and the noise generated by the roof being torn away caused everyone in the room to lose their focus. They stopped and raised their gaze, only to witness the ceiling quickly follow.

As they stared though the gaping hole, they weren't confronted with the expected chaos and airborne debris, but a clear sky, which they later described as serene.

The storm peaked and although the contractions had stopped, Ellen had an overwhelming urge to push.

At exactly 16:18, their daughter was born.

The normal procedure was to clean up the baby and give it to the mother, but under the circumstances, Ellen didn't get to hold her until later. The baby was put into a wheeled plastic bassinet so they could rush her off to get her checked over in a safer part of the hospital.

As they were preparing to leave, there was a flurry of snowflake-like ice particles falling through the void of the storm vortex. They weren't white like snow, but crystal clear ice.

Moments before it set, the fading light of the sun shone through the particles, refracting with the intensity of the purest diamond. It was the intensity of the purple shining directly on the baby that made them, once again, stare towards the heavens.

Although it went on for over a minute, the outside temperature was so cold they should have fallen to the floor, but they dissipated before entering the building.

Everyone in the room was in awe of this odd phenomenon and as they stared upwards, a larger solitary ice flake glistened and sparkled as it descended.

However, this didn't dissipate at the same height as the others. Due to its size, it should have fallen like a rock but it gently floated downwards, growing smaller and smaller, until it could barely be seen.

It landed in the middle of the baby's forehead, discharging a small static crackle and spark.

As it melted away, it left a ghostly imprint of a mandala with a figure eight infinity symbol at its centre.

With a thunderous roar, a lightning bolt followed. The dusky sky lit up and the intense light blinded them for a few seconds as it followed an almost pre-determined path through the delivery suite doors to the feet of the porter.

A brief smile brushed the baby's lips as she momentarily opened her eyes.

Doors still ajar, they could see the porter at the end of the corridor initially lying motionless, then, without the aid of his arms, he rose from the floor, walked towards them and entered the suite.

The hospital staff knew him as a quiet, nervous and introverted man, but this time there was something different. His presence was emanating and they felt something truly great.

As he approached, the doors of the suite opened fully. They were in awe of the air of divinity and love he carried with him.

He proceeded towards the baby, kissed the imprint on her forehead and left.

The staff never saw him again.

On his departure, as if with a heavenly hand, the eye of the storm had been seized and elevated out of existence with such force, it lifted them off their feet.

Speechless and shaken, they resumed their care of Ellen and took the baby for observations. On completion, the child was reunited with her mother.

Consumed with love and gratitude for the safe arrival of their daughter, they began to discuss names. Morty had no idea nor preference and said he was happy for Ellen to choose the name, until she said she wanted to name her after the storm.

"That's ludicrous. We can't burden her with that. And what do you think people would say?" he said. "Did you hear what the hippies named their daughter? No, no, no, we can't do that to her."

But he came around eventually due to Ellen's insistence.

Surprisingly, there was no other damage to the hospital and only minor damage to surrounding buildings caused by the flying debris of the hospital roof, and after being predicted as the worst storm in recorded history, it passed with little of the devastation assured by the Meteorological Service of Canada.

Eerily precise in its path, the winds reached unimaginable speeds and those brave or foolish enough to risk being outside to bear witness described it as a pulsating column of wind, water and debris, dramatically changing in diameter and not always in contact with the ground. One moment, it was brewing a few feet from the ground, the next it was roaring amongst the clouds.

Though it had passed, it wasn't over yet.

Joseph

METEOROLOGICAL SERVICE OF CANADA, AUGUST 30

16 MONTHS EARLIER

Joseph had finished his seventh and final forecast and still the gut feeling just wouldn't leave.

From the core of his being, he knew this wasn't the end of it, but even he was surprised by what the forecast model threw up.

As well as many other global weather patterns, meteorological offices worldwide were monitoring the severe situation in British Columbia. All staffed with very experienced analytical personnel, yet none nearly as diligent as Joseph.

With his forecast complete, he sat there dumbstruck. He could not believe what the visual was showing him. He was right about the smaller storm centres. They were still active.

He had the visual on loop and watched intently trying to absorb and analyse what was before him. The smaller storm centres reappeared sequentially, circling and edging away from the storm's eye whilst pulsating in and out of view. The pattern of circling had a mathematical familiarity to it, but no matter how hard he tried, he couldn't recall it.

Considering the hours already spent on the previous forecasts, he wondered whether or not this would have been the result if he had prolonged forecast six.

Still very confident with his findings, Joseph made another visit to the director's office. He was apprehensive but he couldn't not go.

Once loaded onto the thumb drive, he turned off his computer. This, he had never done before. All devices were turned off only at the end of the day, and sometimes not even then.

After knocking on the door, he heard the director say enter, but the look on his face made him even more apprehensive and a gut feeling surfaced. He knew this wouldn't end as he'd hoped.

"What now, Joseph?" said the director in a stern annoyed tone.

With a stutter, Joseph began to explain.

Antonis humoured him initially and allowed him to continue for a couple of minutes, but as the director had made up his mind as soon as he saw who was at his door, he cut Joseph off mid-sentence. Antonis told him to report to HR first thing the following morning. As Joseph was contracted annually, there was no legal issue surrounding the end of his employment.

With concerns still eating away at him, Joseph decided on one final forecast.

Sat in front of his Mac, he sat patiently as it started up. Aware of the symbolic nature of the Apple logo, he sensed the weather situation was far bigger than just the storm.

He entered enough data for the visual to last over a minute, pressed play and watched intently. The thirty-two-inch screen displayed the visual with such vibrancy he was becoming entranced once again. The first fifty seconds showed the same storm formation, followed by the sequential appearance of the six smaller storm eyes.

From what he'd seen so far, his expectation was for the storm centres to amalgamate.

They did.

Now assuming he'd been wrong all along, Joseph reached for the mouse to close the application. As he moved the cursor from the bottom right corner over the visual to the close button in the top left, he saw them emerge once again.

He resisted closing the application and the result revealed itself.

At a specific point circling the eye, each smaller one ejected itself and travelled the path of an ever-increasing arc.

He watched until the last of the smaller storm centres left.

All arcs were the same, but the point at which they were ejected determined their trajectory.

Each one reached its peak over every one of the other six continents.

With the dressing down he'd received from Mr Backlav, he knew it would be foolish to attempt to convince him again. It was worse than even he had thought. The storms were headed to devastate all seven continents. Unfortunately, there was no one else he could speak to; he was the only one who knew of this, and it stayed that way.

His contract wasn't renewed and after coming to terms with what happened, he suffered extreme depression. He couldn't face the self-imposed pressure that accompanied him at the office and decided to take time out from meteorology and took a short-term unqualified position as a porter at the local hospital.

He kept this job until the storm he was so sure of had passed.

CREATION

Crystal

We have known each other for over forty years now, and in retrospect, we realised how important it was that we never told anyone of the capabilities of our balls. It was a pact we made when we all first met.

Being very young and prior to our first meeting, we did tell our parents of some adventures but as they mostly happened during the early hours of the morning, they were not dismissed but believed to be and treated as dreams.

Had we spoken of them at an age where we were insistent it wasn't dreaming, we would have had very different lives. As far as we were aware at that time, we were the only ones.

If there were others, they obviously never spoke of it either.

I was born on January 16 at 4:18 in the afternoon to Morty and Ellen. The only child of older than normal first-time parents. The day I was born was very strange indeed. To everyone, it was an odd phenomenon and I remember it all.

Not just my birth but also my incarnation.

Creation could be interpreted as a lot of effort, but I understood the laws of the universe and it was the effortless natural progression of my internal intent.

Historical reports of children who remembered their births and previous incarnations, together with the evidence that supported their claims, were undeniable. The interest in those children was initially very curious and intense, yet their claims were never really taken seriously, regardless of the evidence. Some were examined and questioned in depth by scholars and professors, but their stories were debunked.

Parents were told it was "a vivid imagination" and "a phase they were going through which would soon pass".

It was unfortunate they were never taken seriously. Had they been, they could have become the key to a far better understanding of our spirit within.

We all played our part and, for me, it began with a desire to be. For Mum, it was the desire for a child, while for Dad it was that raw carnal desire; although, were it not for that basic instinct of his, I would not be in this time-space reality.

I could have been the child of anyone, anywhere, anytime, but as the universe always does, in symphonic harmony, it arranged all compatible genetics and desires to collaborate at the exact moment.

There I was.

A thought amongst countless others in my father's mind and, as always, I wasn't the only one ready for this part, but I was the only one with the focus, determination and least resistance to get where I needed to be.

My consciousness was so focused, it began to attract the genetically coded DNA necessary for my unmanifested consciousness to gain physical presence.

Over time, my consciousness became cocooned within the physical matter of DNA, in the form of what looked like a tadpole, in preparation for the onwards journey.

Creation is an adventure in itself and scientists in laboratories around the world have tried many times to create that initial spark of life, legally and illegally, but it's not something that can be created outside of the natural biological processes.

I understood what they didn't. All earthly life forms are a non-physical consciousness cocooned within a physical presence.

I became the seed and Dad's desire was in the offing. There was to be a thunderous rush towards the destination and it would be the beginning of what Mum so desperately desired.

In microscopic physical form, all thoughts were now manifest.

The union began and, with that critical point moving ever closer, the sudden burst of energy propelled every seed forwards.

They raced frantically onwards, but I let them pass, gently meandering at my own pace. Exerting the energy I held in a prolonged manner in order to reach the destination first was foolish.

I felt it was mine for the taking.

Along the journey, there were many I passed that didn't have the stamina to continue and when I arrived, the egg remained unfertilised.

Though many tried, it was waiting for me.

That was the moment I needed the energy I had conserved.

The tail of a sperm has a small surface area, so the necessary violent thrashing generated the appropriate amount of thrust to succeed.

It worked. I entered the egg and began the process of creation.

The foremost thought on my mind was how my body would become what I intended it to be.

Once the fission began, prior to the development of the body, I focused on the chakras. Though there are one hundred and fourteen in all, a lot of time and energy went on the seven centres; the first being the root.

By the time I completed the first six, my focus was so sharp my crown chakra couldn't have been more precise.

To explain this process in a way humanity could understand is virtually impossible as currently there is no vocabulary to explain or comprehend it in its entirety.

I won't go into detail but suffice to say, I found the wiring of the brain the most challenging. Only now do I understand why some connections wired differently to what they should have been, but then that's what makes me me, and I later learnt the other six had similar complications.

I was extremely grateful for my different ability.

Creation! What a great time I had with that.

I was the last person to join the group because my dominant chakra was the crown. However, our group had a root, and this was Amelia's dominant chakra.

Amelia

I was born January 16 at 16:18 in Patagonia. Though Mum and Dad were British by birth, they relocated many times with Dad's job.

He was in the air force and Mum was a teacher. Both were very successful in what they did, but were still climbing the ladder to become better at what they did, so they could give me a stable and loving family life.

Dad began his career in the RAF. He was exceptionally good at his job, and was eventually made an offer he couldn't refuse.

They migrated to Australia and he joined the RAAF. Opportunities abounded and he had many promotions during his time there. He was a visionary within his job and very highly thought of. As a consequence, he was offered a position on the international exchange programme as a flight instructor with the Argentine Air Force, operating out of Patagonia.

Mum wasn't sure about taking this two-year posting because they were planning their family, and the choice was either: put off my conception or have me in South America. After many discussions, they decided on the latter. I was conceived in the May, two months prior to their move.

They settled quickly and made many friends. Dad got straight into his work, and from day one Mum says he spent more time there than he needed to.

It wasn't worth Mum trying to get a job at the university because of her pregnancy. She said there wouldn't be enough continuity in it for either her or the students, so she decided on private tutoring for English-speaking maths students. But only having students for a couple of hours a week, she went stir crazy occasionally.

Knowing Mum would need all the support she could get, Dad intended to take paternity leave when I was born.

Due to the requirements of the position he held, Dad always checked the meteorology website and knew of the storm prior to their journey. The closest it would get to them was twenty miles, so he decided to take Mum out for the day to break the monotony she was feeling.

The surprise took her a little off guard and felt almost pressured to get ready. In a hurried manner, she scanned her wardrobe. Amongst the compacted hanging clothes, the brightly coloured shoulder of a dress was protruding. Unable to recall this item of clothing, she eventually parted the masses of material to access it.

It was perfect.

Made for the occasion, she thought.

They had to set off early as he intended to make a fuss of her the whole day and make it unforgettable. He planned to take her to an art gallery and museum, finishing with a picnic at her favourite spot.

He packed the car with the picnic blanket and hamper he had prepared all by himself with smoked salmon sandwiches, some French cheeses, grapes, a couple of beers for him and some fizzy elderflower cordial for her, but what started as a beautiful sunny day ended very differently.

Mum said she was surprised by his romanticism and, up until the storm, it was one of the best days she'd had with Dad.

After a wonderful day together, they made their way back home.

Not half an hour into their journey, he noticed it in his rear-view mirror. The storm was closer than his regularly visited weather channels and websites predicted and it seemed to be following them.

The black sky that was so far away was gaining fast, soon to be right above them. The storm had taken a different path to that predicted by the meteorologists, and this concerned Dad.

It began with heavy rain, then hail the size of golf balls. Falling hard and spiralling within the twisting wind, it dented every panel of the car.

Behind them in the distance, Dad saw four twisters that appeared to be bouncing, occasionally making ground fall. They were so ferocious they eventually blended together to make one large twister. Mum said she felt a dramatic change in atmospheric pressure and believed this was instrumental in starting the contractions and the eventual breaking of her waters. Very little panicked Dad, but that day was an exception.

Being a practical man, he realised how impossible it would be for Mum to give birth in such a small car and by this time, the streets were deserted so no help was available even if he wanted it. He knew the responsibility of birthing me lay squarely on his shoulders.

Through the driving rain, and barely visible through the windshield, he saw a bus shelter ahead of them. Slowly, he drove towards it. Hoping the car would shield them from the storm, he parked as close as he could on the pavement, marginally missing the shelter.

There was a medical centre at the air base, but they were forty miles away, and the nearest hospital was thirty-eight miles in the opposite direction.

With the wind, rain and hail so intense, and poor visibility to boot, they knew neither were options they could consider.

Time was a major factor.

Dad got out of the car and with the sun blazing down on him, he looked around. Everything was eerily calm. He looked up. Not to clear blue skies, but the centre of the twister which was half a kilometre wide. He couldn't see outside the walls of it due to the density of rain, hail and debris; yet, instead of it sucking everything up from the centre, warm air was being blown down.

Unsure how long it would last, they were thankful for the calm.

Still on edge, neither of them had witnessed a storm of this ferocity before, and the ensuing devastation could only be guessed at.

Would it be long enough to give birth?

He went to the boot for the picnic blanket, then he went to get Mum out and sat her on the bench while he laid out the blanket. Though initially pressured into choosing her attire, the spacious loose flowing dress made it easier for them whilst preparing her to give birth.

Once she was comfortable, he got out his mobile and called the emergency services. He calmly explained the situation and gave their location. He was told that there would be an ambulance there as soon as possible, but they couldn't give an estimated time of arrival due to the weather, so as a backup, he called the air base. They also dispatched an ambulance.

No sooner had he finished on the phone, Mum began screaming and cursing at him. The contractions had restarted and were coming quickly. With no idea of what to do, he just did what he'd seen on TV, telling her to breathe and push.

Luckily for him, it was over in about three minutes. He took off his wet coat, then his dry T-shirt and wrapped me in it and gave me to Mum. He hurried to the back of the car, opened the picnic hamper and retrieved the grape scissors.

Once I had been detached, the twister began to bounce again. They looked up, only to be confronted with the largest hailstone they'd ever seen and it was heading straight for them. Though they worried initially, the closer it grew, the smaller it became.

My right arm was hanging out of the T-shirt I was wrapped in. The hailstone fell, diminished to virtually nothing, and landed in the palm of my hand. Mum said I let out an almighty scream.

The reason for this wasn't the impact, but the static within. The hailstone had absorbed an unusual amount and on contact with my hand, it discharged everything it held and left a tiny scar in the shape of what looked like a coffin.

Because I was crying so inconsolably, they didn't notice the dissipation of the storm as the twister gently raised back up. Their attention eventually diverted to the arrival of two ambulances, one from the hospital and the other from the air base.

The medics from the hospital ambulance took control. They cleaned me up and checked me over, then tended to Mum. We were put into the ambulance to take us to hospital and Dad followed in the car.

When news got out of the circumstances surrounding my birth, my parents were harassed for a while. Journalists from most news channels wanted a story.

The rest of their time in Patagonia was pretty uneventful.

At the age of eighteen months, we moved back to Australia. Mum got a job teaching maths at the university where she reacquainted with her friends Sharon and Sandie. Dad was promoted to commanding officer at the flight training school, where he met Daigo, a Japanese pilot, on the international exchange programme.

The "why" phase that children go through normally begins at two years of age whereas mine began as soon as I was able to string sentences together, and within months of meeting Daigo, a very apparent change took place.

Dad began to answer my questions differently.

He used to answer them in a way that he knew all the answers, but now he would almost insist that I questioned his answers.

Whenever I had any questions for my parents, the answer would often begin with, "My answer will not be the truth, but my opinion. It will be my truth, but if the answer is that important to you, then you should ask other people too. Only then can you decide what is true for you."

My parents believed it was better for us to decide for ourselves and change our minds as we grew, rather than wait until we were older and realise the beliefs we held weren't our own or wrong for us.

They were very wise.

I was very fortunate to have been brought up this way. I was given the freedom to make my own decisions. Not just on what I did, but what I chose to believe. It worked out well for Claudia too as she had always been treated this way.

In part, it helped with her transition into our family, though with the news of my slowly deteriorating hearing, it was a very trying time for Mum and Dad.

Daigo had already been in the position for a year when Dad met him, but from day one, they became very close as did Mum and Daigo's wife, Holly. The reason for this was firstly, they had a daughter who was born in Japan on the same day as me, but what he thought was spooky about it was that she was born under similar circumstances during the global storm of that year. They became inseparable.

Sharon and Sandi or "the Shandies" as we called them, welcomed Mum's new friend Holly with open arms and they, as a group of six, always socialised together.

Daigo's exchange was a two-year posting initially, but after one year in Australia, they loved it so much Holly asked Daigo if there was any way they could stay for longer.

He enquired about extending the exchange, and after six months back in Japan at the end of his first posting, he was authorised to take a second posting there with the agreement of the RAAF.

Life was pretty normal until my fifth birthday. Day care, kindy and then school, holidays, picnics, play dates. All the good stuff.

Christmas of the year prior to my fifth birthday, apart from the usual girly stuff, I had an unusual ball as a present. Dad was a bit of a gadget freak, and I think it was really for him, but he thought I might enjoy playing with this unusual piece of technology.

Not knowing what it was or what it was supposed to do, if anything, I had a go. I played with it and it kept my attention for about three minutes.

I quickly became bored and didn't touch it until Claudia came to stay.

Claudia

I was the only daughter of a Japanese fighter pilot and an American missionary. Dad was studying in America and he met Mum on one of her rare visits home, after months at a time volunteering somewhere obscure in the world.

It was a regular Saturday morning for him. Up early, gym, home, shower, shopping.

Their meeting was accidental.

Dad reversed into the front of her car in the supermarket car park.

Tired from the gym and shopping, his attention wasn't on his driving. After loading his shopping in the boot, he jumped in and started the car; his mind on what he would have for lunch as he began to reverse.

He cursed his new shoes when his right foot slipped off the brake onto the accelerator.

After the bump, he re-parked in the same spot and reached into the glove box for a pen and paper, and wrote a note with his contact details.

When he realised he was writing in Japanese, he tore the paper from the pad and threw it in the door pocket. Sat thinking of the correct translation, he noticed people watching him. He assumed they were waiting to see if he was going to leave the scene and drive off.

Some onlookers were holding up their phones, taking pictures, videoing him and his car, in the event he left.

He opened his car door and, as he stood up, he saw a rather large menacing-looking man heading straight towards him as if to confront him and get his details. But, as he approached, Dad made his way to Mum's car and tucked the note under the wiper. The man promptly turned on his heels and returned to his own car to help his wife load their shopping.

Carefully pulling out of his space once again, in his rear-view mirror, he noticed a petite young woman walk to the back of the car he'd bumped. He re-entered his parking space, turned off the engine and exited the car once again.

He made his way towards her.

Getting ready to load her shopping, she looked up and saw a man walking in her direction.

Here we go again, she thought.

She couldn't understand why, but wherever she went, however she looked, she always attracted the attention of men.

Devoid of makeup, she turned.

Her natural beauty floored him.

He was speechless initially, but words eventually managed to stumble from his mouth.

Being a humble and polite man, he explained the situation and asked for her details so he could pass them on to his insurers.

She obliged.

Though not that unusual, it was a surprise to him that they were both insured with the same company.

On listening to Dad, she felt a little guilty at her presumptions and smiled at him.

There was a definite spark between them.

She went to the front of her car to see the damage. To her, it looked quite minor, but as they were stood discussing it, Dad noticed the water trickling from underneath.

Before he could say anything, she said, "That's no problem, we'll let the insurance companies deal with it," and thanked him for his honesty.

Being mechanically minded, he knew she wouldn't get far with a leaking radiator, and more damage would be done if she drove home, so he pointed this out to her and offered to take her, and her shopping, home.

As she had many things to do that day, she cautiously accepted his offer.

He held out his hand and coyly said, "I'm Daigo."

With a demure smile, she shook his hand and said, "Holly."

Her apartment was a twenty-minute drive from the supermarket and to Dad's surprise, they only lived a mile apart.

That drive was instrumental to their lives and, subsequently, mine.

After the usual questions of what they did for a living and where they were from, upbringing became the topic that interested Mum.

She was schooled and lived in a very religious setting. The children's home's charter was bordering on the extreme. She was never allowed to question anything she was taught.

Dad, on the other hand, was encouraged to question everything.

They discussed this in depth and Mum said if she was to ever have children, that was how she would bring them up. To know their own minds and question everything, and not follow the crowd like sheep.

As they went deeper, their parting conversation ended on a less cheery note.

They had a common bond.

They were both orphaned as very young children with no other known family.

There they were, two orphans sat outside an apartment block, about to become the love of each other's lives.

Dad said he would get on to the insurance company straight away to see if they could arrange for her car to be towed back to her apartment or picked up and taken to a garage that day, so it wouldn't be left in the car park indefinitely.

He helped her upstairs with her shopping and asked if she would be okay and if there was anything else he could do for her.

"Where do I begin?" she said with a smirk on her face. "First, I have to go to the doctors this afternoon, and probably the pharmacy after that. Then I'm volunteering at a homeless shelter at six, then I have to get back home afterwards. Tomorrow, the soup kitchen is moving to a new location and they may want me there. I think that's going to be a long day. I'm supposed to be there at one and they said they may not finish till eight, but they always call the night before to confirm if they need me or not."

He noted in his mobile phone:

First, doctors

6 p.m. take to homeless shelter

Tomorrow

1 p.m. at soup kitchen

8 p.m. pick up (maybe earlier)

He always looked forward to a lie in on a Sunday morning, but was more than happy to ferry her around. It was a public holiday weekend and had no plans, which was lucky for him as Mum needed transport for her appointments and volunteer work over those two days.

Dad suggested he be her chauffeur until her courtesy car arrived from the insurance company.

With a smile on her face, she very happily agreed to this.

It was only eleven minutes past eleven by this time, and Mum's appointment at the medical centre wasn't until half past two, so Dad said he would take his shopping back to his house, which he shared with others, and he would be back to pick her up.

As he turned to leave, his name jumped out of her mouth.

He looked back.

They made eye contact and they knew they were thinking the same thing. She couldn't bring herself to do it, but she had the most intense urge to kiss him goodbye.

"Oh, nothing," she said, but they both had that knowing smile.

He said, "I'll be back in about an hour."

Strangely comfortable in each other's company, they felt like more than old friends, and from the moment he left, they couldn't stop thinking of each other.

As he closed the door, she had the biggest smile on her face. She had never felt like this before.

Boyfriends were not something she was ever really interested in. She was an independent compassionate woman, and the drive in her life was helping others.

She grabbed her shopping and took it to the kitchen, and as she began to put it away, she realised it was only just after eleven, and her appointment at the doctors, which was only a ten-minute drive away, meant they would have a lot more time together. Although she was unsure of his motives, she was quite excited by the thought of spending more time with him.

He was a good-looking man and very charming, but what got her was the gentlemanly air about him.

Dad couldn't stop smiling; he was almost skipping down the stairs from her apartment. He knew he would marry this woman.

He got into his car and started the engine and the radio came on. He didn't know the song playing, but as he listened to the lyrics, he laughed to himself because they mostly described how he was feeling and the fact it was called "Written in the Stars" blew his mind a little.

As soon as he got home, he put away his groceries, and then called the claim line of his insurance company, Port House Insurance. Surprisingly, they were more than helpful, and it only took him fifteen minutes. He explained what had happened and asked if it would be possible to get the car collected today.

He was told the third party would have to contact their insurance company to arrange that. Dad then informed the lady on the phone the third party was insured with them too.

After taking Dad's details and his account of what happened, PHI 1111-1-618033 was the reference number he was to give to the third party and once reported, details would be passed onto their nominated repairer. They would contact the third party in due course, but could not guarantee the collection of the car today.

On completing the call, he poured a glass of water, took a sip then made his way over to Mum's.

Once her shopping was put away, she took a shower and put on something a little tidier than her tracksuit bottoms and T-shirt.

She finally decided on her red and cream flowery dress and beige flat shoes. She wasn't normally a girly type, but when she wanted to, she could carry it off well.

The intercom buzzed.

Mum pressed the button and said, "Hello?"

"Hi Holly. It's Daigo."

"Come on up," she said, and promptly buzzed him in.

As he walked through the door, they both felt the heat between them; there was a definite chemistry.

Dad gave her the reference number and told her what the insurance company said and she called them straight away. She was told the garage would contact her to exchange keys, and they would arrange a courtesy car.

The Coffee House was just a few minutes' walk from the doctors and, having quite a bit of time before her appointment, they decided to go for coffee and a bite to eat.

There was a lot of laughter as they shared snippets of stories from their past to their career choices and goals. Time passed quickly and before they knew it, it was time for her appointment.

At ten minutes to three, Mum came out of the doctors and everything was fine so the trip to the pharmacy was no longer necessary.

They made their way back to Mum's place when the phone rang. It was the garage. She was told the car would be collected at four, so they decided to go to the supermarket car park and wait for the tow truck.

The sight of the dilapidated flatbed truck billowing smoke from the exhaust didn't instil confidence in the forthcoming repairs.

They promptly exited the car and directed the truck to Mum's car. With no other vehicle accompanying the truck, Mum asked about the courtesy car.

"All have been allocated until Tuesday. You probably won't get the courtesy car until then. Or Wednesday at the latest because of the public holiday. But if you or your husband call the garage first thing Tuesday morning and be firm with them, they should be able to accommodate you."

She wasn't sure whether to be annoyed at the fact he didn't think she could be firm with people, or laugh because he thought they were married, but she politely smiled and agreed with him, all the while looking forward to spending more time with Dad.

After laughing together about their assumed marriage, they made their way back.

Not wanting their time together to end, Dad suggested they go out on a date that night. Mum agreed, but said it couldn't be a late one as she would probably be working at the soup kitchen on Sunday.

At six forty-five, he'd arrived early, and the slow deep jazz tones of the radio station only added to his eager anticipation of Mum's appearance.

After discussing their food likes and dislikes, they decided on KULCHA, a small Asian restaurant just out of town.

They both turned off their phones so as not to be distracted for one moment, and they had the most fabulous time.

As she glanced around the restaurant, she noticed the clock.

"Goodness, it's almost eleven!" Reluctantly, she added, "I really should be getting back."

Remembering her plans, Dad agreed and paid the bill, which Mum appreciated very much.

Once her seatbelt was secured, she reached into her bag and took out her phone. Once powered up, it gave one continuous tone. She knew a tone that long meant a lot of messages or missed calls. It had six missed call, one message and eight text messages. There was one call from the soup kitchen manager. The rest were from her friend Angie.

She promptly accessed her voicemail to retrieve it.

Dad waited for her to finish the call before starting the engine and, as he watched her, admiring every aspect of her, she had the biggest smile appear on her face and without a word she began to read Angie's messages.

"That looked like it was good news," Dad said as he started the car.

Still smiling whilst trying to contain her excitement, she continued to scroll through the messages from Angie.

"Oh. No, it was just my friend asking me about how it was going and making silly comments." Not wanting to sound too keen, she turned and said, "How do you fancy going on to a bar or a club?"

Surprised by this, he said, "I'm not sure that's a good idea…"

Before he could finish his sentence, her face dropped.

Surely he's had as good as time as I have? Why doesn't he want to continue our evening? Did I say anything to upset him? she thought.

Confused by the look on her face he finished his sentence. "… You have to be up so early tomorrow."

With relief on her face, she replied, "Oh. No. The voice message was from the manager of the soup kitchen saying he didn't need me tomorrow. They've had a number of people over the last week contact them to see if they needed any more volunteers."

Frequenting a number of bars and clubs, their time together was filled with dancing and laughter. They had an unforgettable evening.

Being a true gentleman, at the end of the night, he dropped her off at her apartment and saw her to the door. Being the lady she was, she kissed him on the cheek and promised to call him the following day.

Every moment they were apart, all they could do was think of each other.

They spent all of Monday and Tuesday together, and were now officially an item.

Dad took the morning off from university on the Tuesday to sort out Mum's courtesy car, and within two weeks, she had her car back.

After an incident that could have been such a disaster, Dad said everything went so smoothly, and they had the most fantastic time together. It really was as if it was written in the stars.

I loved hearing Dad tell the story of their meeting. To me, it seemed he was re-living it every time he told me, never missing a thing. Not even the minutest detail.

Amelia

The day my sister came home with us was a bittersweet day for us all. It all happened just before our fifth birthday.

When they thought I was old enough, Mum and Dad told me in great detail of Daigo and Holly's accident. Whenever I think back to the events of that day, I wonder if all of that devastation for Daigo, Holly and Claudia was down to fate.

The air force crew were scheduled to do an afternoon flypast for New Year's Eve day celebrations prior to the firework display at night.

There were nine aircraft in the formation and though performed many times in the past, they still practiced the Diamond Nine prior to the event as it wasn't always the same pilots involved in this spectacle.

It was two and a half months before Holly, Daigo and Claudia were to return to Japan, and as Dad was the commanding officer of the squadron, he managed to get authorisation from Air Marshall Frisina, the chief of the air force, for all pilots to take their spouses on the practice formation.

Prior to the flights, they each underwent a medical to ensure they were fit to fly and able to endure the extreme G forces that these aircraft could achieve. They were all very excited about flying in these propellor driven aircraft, because it was a rare opportunity for spouses and partners alike.

I would normally have been at home with Mum, and Claudia would have been at home with Holly, but as they were both out on a jolly with Dad and Daigo the previous night, we stayed with Mum's friends, the Shandies.

I occasionally stayed over at the Shandies' due to my weekly sign language lessons and, over a period of time, I commandeered my own room due to the number of things I left there. Even so, I still took more toys with me that day, because Claudia was coming too.

We had a great time together. Sharon and Sandie were like our adoptive mothers and they always treated us as their own.

Mum and Dad were up early that day as their take-off time was seven in the morning.

They arrived at the air base by five thirty, so Dad had time to go through the flight plan with the pilots, and follow protocol prior to taking the aircraft. Safety was paramount.

Although the flypast procedure lasted less than two minutes from the formation to the actual flypast, their schedule allowed them an hour, which gave them up to forty five minutes to take their passengers on an aerial tour of the city and follow the river through the valleys, and show them a part of what their job entailed. Sick bags were always provided, and by demonstrating their aerobatic abilities, attempts were always made for passengers to use them.

Everybody had a great time. The practice flypast was accurate to the second and everyone was pleased everything had gone to plan without a hitch; the day had gone so well. This ended an exceptional experience for the passengers and they made their way back to base.

Punctual as always, it was 8 a.m. exactly when Dad's wheels touched down. Pete and Siv followed, then Daigo and Holly.

Daigo approached the runway in the same manner as always, but came in with a slightly heavier landing, but nothing unusual. The aircraft were built to withstand this to a certain degree.

Dad and Pete had already parked under the hangar and were disembarking as Daigo was travelling along the taxiway. The remaining six aircraft continued with their landings.

The four of them turned to the sound of an explosion.

Something was seriously wrong.

Expecting to see an aircraft in flames on the runway, they were confronted with a stomach-churning view. Both ejector seats had activated in Daigo's aircraft.

They stood, staring in disbelief.

They watched helplessly as Daigo and Holly plummeted to the ground. Their parachutes deployed, but the altitude was too low for them to fully open.

Within a minute, fire engines and ambulances were tearing along the taxiway. The firemen stood in preparation for any eventuality with the aircraft, whilst the medics tended to Daigo and Holly.

Knowing the possible outcomes from such a violent expulsion, the paramedics were cautious during their assessment of the situation. Though dazed and confused, Daigo was conscious but due to his concussion, he was unaware of his surroundings and what had just taken place.

He was moving his head a lot, trying to scan his surroundings but the medics were worried. He wasn't moving any other part of his body and their questions were met with incoherent responses.

Apart from being unable to move, he displayed no superficial injuries. The paramedics knew an explosion of that magnitude whilst seated put immense pressure on the spine, so after carefully releasing him from the seat, he was put on a stretcher and taken to the ambulance.

En route to the medical facility, and only able to move his head, he glanced through the ambulance window to see more people heading towards something on the ground. In his confusion, he knew nothing of what had just occurred.

No more flights would commence that day. The firemen cordoned off the aircraft and the area where the seats impacted, while the medics attended to Holly.

There was a stillness to her. They checked for a pulse. It was there, but very faint.

All precautions were taken as they released her from the seat and moved her to the ambulance. Unconscious, she was taken directly to the public hospital as the air base wasn't equipped to deal with her condition. After some tests, Daigo too was taken there.

It all happened in a moment with no time to assume the correct posture for the explosive ejection. Though he remained conscious, Daigo suffered four broken vertebrae. Unfortunately, there were far more serious consequences for Holly.

To the disappointment of the public, the much-anticipated flypast was cancelled last minute as all aircraft of that type were grounded until a full investigation was carried out.

Claudia and I had so much fun that day. Mum took me over early evening and Claudia was already there. Mum went to the kitchen with Sharon and I went to the game room with Claudia.

She was shaking something in her hand and it was flashing lights. It looked familiar and I asked her about it. She stopped and showed me. She told me her parents played a lot of tennis and her dad recently bought the ball to help strengthen his serve, but she enjoyed playing with it so much, he gave it to her.

It was a steel wheel encased in a spherical plastic outer casing with an opening at the bottom and a digital display on top. I had one too but hadn't seen it for a while. I was excited to try it again because mine never worked like that.

The slight protrusion of the wheel allowed for the insertion of a string into a small hole. She gave it to me, wound on the string and quickly pulled. After a couple of attempts, I had it spinning. With gentle rotations of my wrist, it spun faster and the lights began to glow. The invisible silent force it emitted made my wrist and arm ache, but I kept it going for as long as my arm would allow.

It was mesmerising.

We searched through the things I had left there and eventually found mine. After many attempts, I was almost as good as her. I did drop it many times at first as the force was too overpowering. The ache it gave me made me want to stop but she convinced me otherwise.

We had a late night, watching Disney films with Sharon and Sandi, and when we finally went to bed, we were too tired to play with the balls again so we put them on the side. Apart from waking to open the window due to the heat, we slept well that night.

Five minutes after eight, I was awoken by an incessant twitch below my eye. As I opened my eyes, I thought I saw a decreasing ball of light split and enter both balls. It happened so quickly I sometimes feel I may have dreamt it.

I sat up and began to push hard on the top of my cheek to make the twitching stop, but it wouldn't.

With anxiety building, I woke Claudia. I gently shook her.

She opened her eyes, looked at me and said, "Wow, you look amazing."

My attention was now diverted from the twitch. I wondered what she meant.

"What?" I asked.

"You have a bright colour all around you."

"What do you mean?"

"The light coming from your body, it looks really nice."

I didn't mention the twitch as it had stopped, but I eventually learnt it was a warning sign.

From that day forward, she saw colours emanating from everyone. It was novel to her at first, but after a while, it became normal and she only mentioned it when there was something very different. She soon learnt what it was and how it could help her.

With hindsight, the timings of these events were no coincidence.

Mum and Dad were late, and when they eventually arrived to collect me, Daigo and Holly weren't with them.

They were trying very hard to conceal their emotions but they had obviously been crying.

Mum came in first and gave us both a hug. It was one like no other. It wasn't how tightly she squeezed us but the emotion emanating from her. It was palpable.

As we went to the other room to continue playing, Claudia said to me, "Your mum and dad were a funny colour."

"They looked okay to me," I said.

"No, not their faces. It was like your colour earlier, but theirs wasn't just one. There were a lot of colours mixing together."

At the time, neither of us understood what Claudia was witnessing and thought nothing more of it. Mum and Dad went to the kitchen and shared with Sharon and Sandi the dreadful news.

Claudia came home with us that day, initially on a temporary basis. Until Holly had recovered and Daigo's condition improved, they said.

Unfortunately, it never did. He was paralysed from the neck down and little did we know at the time, Holly's condition would continue many years into the future. With Daigo's condition, there was no way he could care for Claudia alone, so once they were given the news, without hesitation, Mum and Dad said they would look after her, if that was what Daigo wanted.

They both knew that neither Daigo nor Holly had any other family.

Daigo agreed, and from that day, to me, she was my sister.

Life was good for me and gradually got better for Claudia.

Claudia

The Shandies were good friends of Amelia's parents, Justin and Naomi, and my first night at their house with Amelia was transformative to my life.

I had been living with my new family for two months and things were starting to feel almost normal again. It was a warm Saturday morning. Justin had just arrived back home from his morning run, Naomi was in the kitchen and Amelia and I were in the front room searching through our toy boxes when I found my force ball.

Remembering our night at the Shandies', we began competing with each other to see who could get the highest number on the display and as we held them close to each other to read the results, there was a loud crack.

From the exposed base, a small lightning bolt, trailed by a wispy gold light, shot from mine to hers. Luckily, we didn't get a shock because we were holding the plastic casing and not touching the steel inner wheel.

We were startled at first, then with a relieved laugh, we continued.

This competition became our bedtime ritual, and once we'd finished competing, before going to sleep, we would keep them on the tallboy in our room so as not to go searching the toy box every night.

The following morning, once Justin had showered, Naomi called us all to the dining room. We sat around the table, enjoying our cooked breakfast. Justin and Naomi were having a quiet discussion. Though I wasn't paying attention to them, it seemed to be of importance.

Amelia and I were laughing and talking incessantly between each mouthful of beans, then the mood mellowed.

Nobody said anything for it to change, I could just feel it.

I made eye contact with Naomi.

I could see in her eyes the love she had for me.

"What's wrong, Mum?" This was an inadvertent slip of the tongue, but it brought a beaming smile to her face.

I think this subject was somehow connected to their conversation.

"Are you happy living here with us?" she asked.

"I love living here. I do miss being with Mum and Dad though."

My reply prompted a glance to Justin. He just smiled and continued with his breakfast.

"We miss your mum terribly, but don't give up hope. I'm sure she will get better soon. Before we visit your dad, we can visit your mum today, if you'd like?"

Talking of Mum saddened me, and Naomi always tried to show there was always hope whenever my mood was sombre.

"I can never take the place your mother," she began, "But the fact you think of us as parents… well, that means so much to us both and Millie too."

I thought of my father and I could feel myself welling up, not knowing how he would feel about me calling someone else Dad, but it has never been mentioned since that day.

We went to the hospital to visit Mum, then on the way to Dad's, we dropped Millie at the Shandies'.

Doctors had previously told Justin and Naomi the deterioration in Millie's hearing was slow but steady, and they were expecting her to lose it completely within ten years. Because of this, Millie would go to the Shandies' every Saturday morning to learn sign language and how to lipread accurately.

Their insistence on these lessons meant she rarely came with us when we visited Dad, which was every week without fail. We let ourselves into the house and I could see something wasn't quite right with Dad.

He appeared to be sad.

I didn't know what it was at first, but after Justin's conversation with him, I saw his mood lift a little.

Apart from the public enquiry as to why civilians were in military aircraft, it transpired that an electrical fault with the command ejection system caused the accident.

Dad always blamed himself but Justin shared the findings of the investigation to put his mind at rest. It was official: he had no part in what happened. He was happy about that but behind his kind facial expression, I could feel the resentment rising.

Not wanting him to become more upset than I thought he already was, I asked him to tell me something about Mum.

He always enjoyed telling the story of how they met; it kept his memories of the fun they had together and the love they shared fresh in his mind as she was the love of his life.

When I got a bit older, I often told him of my dream adventures, which began shortly after the lightning bolt incident with the force ball.

A deep thinker and a philosophical man, he always explained my dreams in a way a child of my age could understand. Compassionately, never judging and always telling me to be careful. Almost as if he knew.

Amelia

It wasn't awkward at all when Claudia began calling them Mum and Dad and it quickly became natural. That first time was a very happy day for them both. In fact, it was a very happy day for us all. I'm almost sure that was the catalyst for what was to come that night.

We went to bed as usual and competed with our balls. The spark that happened the first time didn't happen again until that night, but this time there was a difference. It was a lot bigger and the wispy golden light became a thread.

As we surpassed our previous scores of one thousand one hundred and eleven, unbeknown to us, we hit the crucial number.

From an initial spark, a streak of wispy golden electrical energy became visible, shooting from each ball at opposite sides of the room and they met with a blinding flash.

Back then, we didn't know how we ended up where we did, nor did we know how we got back when we woke up the following morning. Though we had the memory of an adventure, I distinctly remember putting our balls back in their usual place before getting into bed. I was unsure if it was a dream or not.

Once the flash disappeared, we found ourselves hurtling along what appeared to be a winding tube with static electricity arcing all around us. We were travelling so fast we could only just breathe and the resistance was constantly pulling at our hair, pulling so hard it felt like our faces were on the verge of being torn away.

It stopped as quickly as it started. Then, nothing.

Woken with a start, we were confronted by the sound of an angry man shouting at us. We opened our eyes.

A tall, overweight, unkempt man scared us out of our wits. We held each other tightly and began to cry. We had no idea where we were. It obviously wasn't our bedroom.

Just after dawn on what we assumed was the following morning, we were inexplicably in unfamiliar surroundings and in the same bed.

A middle-aged, chubby man with jet black hair and a long droopy moustache stood in front of us dressed in what looked like a bedsheet with a belt and almost shaking with anger.

Trying to figure out what was happening, our minds were racing.

"Who are you? What are you doing here?" he shouted.

Struck with fear, our vocal cords were motionless. We didn't know what to say to him. We were dumbfounded. Trying desperately to verbalise our thoughts, he saw our distress and seemed to calm a little.

We pushed ourselves further back in the bed and held each other tighter as he approached.

He repeated himself, with a softer voice than at first, but still scary.

I was still too scared to speak so Claudia answered.

"Claudia and Amelia," she said between sobs.

Though the language was foreign to us, we understood as if the space between us held a translation anomaly, and the same thing happened when we spoke. English left our mouths, but we heard Greek.

"Where are you from? And how did you get into my house?"

We both answered, "I don't know."

It was the only answer that made any sense to us under the strange circumstances.

He approached us, grabbed our hands and forcibly pulled us from the bed. Dressed similarly to him, our loose clothing tore and with our one free hand, we tried to keep ourselves covered.

Dragging us barefooted to the front door, he threw us onto the street.

Looking like two dishevelled orphans, petrified, we sobbed in the street. We had no idea what to do next but we were happy to be out of his presence.

It had only just got light and we were surprised to see so many people about. Many passed us but it was the lady across the street that helped us.

As we stood huddled and crying, without hesitation, the woman who witnessed our eviction motioned for us to come over and in a commanding tone said, "Quickly, quickly, come here."

Even with the stern look on her face, she looked far more welcoming than the man who threw us onto the street, so we ran to her.

She took us into the house and sat us at the table. Seeing our distress, she tried to ask in a calming gentle voice but was unable to manage it.

"What on earth were you doing in Stavros' house?"

"I don't know, we don't remember."

"Did he take you against your will?"

"No. We woke up there this morning. The last we remember, we were at home in our bedroom and the next thing, we were woken by that man shouting at us."

After telling us to stay where we were, she shouted to someone in another room. "Pneuma, come to the kitchen."

She quickly explained what had occurred and said, "I'm going over the road to find out exactly what happened."

She left. Sat at the table waiting for her to return, I noticed Claudia had her ball in her hand.

"You have your ball," I said.

Looking around, she asked, "Where?"

"In your hand."

As I pointed, she noticed mine in my hand.

Oddly, we could see and touch each other's ball, but not our own.

Distracted by the apparent appearance of the balls, we didn't notice the old woman.

An elderly lady dressed in a long cream toga with a golden drape over her right shoulder appeared at the doorway. She made her way towards us.

We made eye contact as she spoke. With a glazed look and kind smile, she said, "You're girls. And two of you."

With a wry smile and surprise in her voice, she muttered something under her breath. It sounded like she said, "Good choice," but I wasn't sure.

We looked at each other, then at her.

"I'm Amelia."

"And I'm Claudia."

Looking at us knowingly, we felt at ease wondering if she could help us.

"And I am Pneuma. You have been in my dreams for many decades, only I assumed it was one and you would have been a boy, especially with what lies ahead." She paused for a while almost as if she was listening to something. "Ah, you are two of seven. Yes. Special children, but you are not of this dimension."

With no idea what she was talking about, we looked at each other confused.

She continued. "I am a member of a little known philosophical society called SPA. Initiated by one of our great philosophers, Aristotle, through the influential teachings of his predecessors Socrates and Plato. This is where I learnt of 'the One' and also where the myth began. The balls you are holding are portals. They allow you to travel within all dimensions of reality."

With her glazed look, we wondered if she was crazy. We didn't fully understand what she was talking about, but she knew something we didn't and could obviously see the balls.

"There is a lot you have to learn and, as time goes on, you will find out many things about yourselves. There are things you will be able to do that no one else can. But you must never let anyone know of these, apart from the other five."

With no inkling there were others, our minds whirred again but before we had time to ask, she quickly continued. It was like she was trying to tell us of our futures in a moment. It was all very hurried.

"Why do you think we can understand each other? You don't speak Greek. I don't speak English," she said, staring, as if to force the answer out of us. "All seven of you are children of little resistance, and sometimes no resistance, and because of this, your link to the source is like no other."

She went on to explain.

"Before we are born, we are source energy and full of potential. It is our desire and lack of resistance that enables the process of becoming to begin. Even though it appears we are separate from our source, we never are. No one or nothing is. Ever.

"Everything and everyone has the connection, but those with little or no resistance become knowingly aware of it and the knowledge and power available to them through it.

"We call it knowledge, but it's the interpretation of vibration, and it is this which allows you to understand and speak other languages. This is just one of the many abilities you all have. You just have to learn what the others are.

"They will come to you the moment you need them, and once you know of them, they are yours eternally. However, this knowledge and power can only be used for good, but you will come to understand this. How old are you now?"

"Almost seven," we replied.

"Hmm. I sense you are very intelligent and though seven is the age, you still seem a little immature for what lies ahead of you."

She rose from her seat and left the room to go outside.

We went to the window to see where she went. We peered through to see her crouched, picking some herbs from the garden, then looking at a pedestal topped with a circle and thin triangular piece of stone set upright.

As she turned, we ran back to our seats.

Walking through the door, she said, "As you aren't aware of the power within the spheres you hold, you don't have very long. You should return soon."

On the verge of tears again, Claudia said, "We don't know how to get back."

She gently took our hands to lead us into another room and noticed my birthmark.

"Ah, the death box," she knowingly muttered under her breath.

She carefully studied it and after much contemplation said, with surprise in her voice, "This is a representation of the Mausoleum at Halicarnassus. Do you know of this?"

I shook my head. I knew what a mausoleum and a coffin was, so I was a little scared when I heard this. I didn't want to die.

"Don't be scared, it's about life, not death. The death box represents rest and recovery. It's preparation to go on, to continue your journey.

"All are important but try to journey with the Manifester wherever possible; he or she will be able to bring about whatever is needed, and when any of you need rest or recovery, they will manifest a strong safe place where you can rest without fear of being disturbed. Like the mausoleum.

"The Mausoleum at Halicarnassus once stood in your world. In our world, it was only completed recently. It's that which resonated with me through your birthmark. Though it no longer exists, you will encounter it, and you will know it when you see it. You are a healer, Amelia."

This resonated with me, so I paid as much attention as I could, but my mind began to wander.

Looking around the room, it occurred to me. The interior of the house was basic; it held nothing modern and no electricity. As I considered our dress, it hit me. We weren't from this time-space reality.

Growing more concerned, the woman continued.

"No doubt you, Claudia, have something too. Let me see your hands." She saw Claudia's birthmark. "What's this?"

"They look like Olympic rings," Claudia replied.

Having no idea what this meant, she looked again and said, "There is a resonance of Zeus here, but the way these rings are linked resonates with more."

After a short pause she said, "Hmm. Prometheus. You will be the creative one. As God of the sky, weather, law, order and fate, Zeus, the king of our gods, had many powers and abilities, yet wasn't known as a creator. He gave the task of creation to Prometheus."

She paused for a while then said, "The links may possibly be to do with the powers Zeus held."

During the conversation, she was taking lengths of cotton and pulling them between her top lip and tongue to moisten them to twist and hold together.

Once she was done, she took from her pocket a small, baguette cut smoky quartz ring and said, "We will meet again, but you should wait for a calling before you use these again. It will be very soon and should happen around your seventh birthday. However, should you need my help, wear this ring and think of me when you use your ball and you will meet with me again. Maybe in another form, time or reality."

She told Claudia to take great care of it as she put it on the middle finger of her left hand. It fitted perfectly and, with the stone turned inward, she felt it in the palm of her hand, always safe in her grasp. It was beautiful and I could see she loved it and didn't want to lose it.

Continuing to a close, she took Claudia's hand, turning it to reveal the lower part of the ball. After a few turns of the wheel within, the pinhole presented itself for her to insert one end of the combined cotton threads and began to wind it on.

"Eventually, you will all have a ring each. They will be of different stones and contain unique powers. You do not need these material things, but a memento will help with the development of your abilities and enforce your belief in yourselves."

Once the cotton was wound on, she quickly pulled it and the ball lit up.

"Now keep it spinning slowly while I start Amelia's."

She then began with mine.

While she was doing this, she partially told us of their purpose.

"These are not play things. They are of great dimensional value and relentlessly sought by most who know of them. Two of whom are believed to be the most revered beings ever to have taken the human form. So, you must always keep them safe.

"They are well documented, yet thought to be mythical because they have never been seen, but myth they are not and their value is not monetary. It is power.

"They can be seen by few outside of your reality, but if anyone can touch them as I do, if they acquire them, they can use them just as you do. You must not allow this to happen.

"This is your portal and it will take you wherever you desire, and your destination is decided by your thoughts. So, be very clear because if negativity takes hold or your mind wanders, it can be hard to overcome, and you will end up in some very challenging situations. So, remember, a clear mind is essential every time you travel."

She continued.

"Also, you must always have at least one of the strings with you so you can start the ball, unless you are with the child that holds the capability ball."

Although we didn't understand what this ball was, we confirmed our understanding.

"Are you ready?" she asked.

"Yes."

"Okay. Breathe in and out, deeply but gently, and think of where you came from."

After about thirty seconds, she said, "Can you see where you're going?"

Thoughts of home flooded our imagination as we simultaneously said, "Yes."

"Keep that thought clear and gradually spin your balls faster. Are you sure you've understood everything?"

Though it was a lot of information for us, we remembered most of it.

The lights in our balls grew brighter than we had noticed before; they were almost blinding.

Before the darkness came, her last words were, "Remember, your thoughts take you places."

On our return, all I could think of was who the other five were, and when we would meet them. But Claudia was more concerned that she could no longer see the ring. I assured her it was there.

Araminter

Foretold many decades before by a shaman, the storm in the January of that year would be a worldwide phenomenon. He prophesied the split would affect all continents and on reaching the north-east coast of Africa, the rain and hail from it would dissipate. The wind would create sandstorms of proportions never seen. His prophecy was, "The winds of change will bring a Muttaqan, (one who remembers their origin in the light and whose identity and power is in other worlds) to the middle world."

As a very late addition to the family, and the youngest of eight, I was the only one born at home. It was during a severe sandstorm. Mum described it as chilling. The constant noise of the sand against the windows was as unbearable as the pain, but the moment I was born, there was silence. She said the wind dramatically stopped, and the sand fell to the ground.

My parents had seven children in relatively quick succession, and by the age of twenty-nine, Mum believed her child bearing days were over.

With little to no disposable income, even debt at times, they teetered on the edge of poverty, believing and relying on the eventuality of Dad's succession through the company to pull them through. It was not swift and they struggled for some time as their family grew.

She wasn't quite seventeen when my eldest brother was born. There are eighteen years between him and myself, and six years between my youngest sister, and even though there were eight of us, I felt like an only child.

As a result of her years of child bearing, Mum had always been a housewife but despite this, they were now quite well off.

Dad was now very successful in real estate, but when their fourth child was born, looking after them became too much for her.

Dad worked such long hours and this, combined with business trips, meant it was no longer viable for Mum alone if their marriage was to survive. A nanny was essential, and although she had help with everything, she insisted on cooking every meal for the family. Mum was very particular with the family diet, especially the herbs. She had a deep belief in their symbolic properties. Throughout our lives, rosemary and sage were prevalent as these symbolised memory and wisdom. She told us it was to assist with our education.

My dietary requirements were different to the others, which I believe stemmed from my creation. I enjoyed the feeling that acid and protein gave me.

Though preferential and not medical, Mum still pandered to them.

Scientific knowledge to date suggested this was a random anomaly relating to the egg or sperm prior to fertilisation. Though this may be the case, it wasn't how I acquired my extra chromosome.

Being the youngest, and because I was different, I took up most of our nanny Rehema's time; so much so, I inadvertently called her mum on a number of occasions. I think I was her favourite.

I spent so much time with her, it was inevitable that she would notice the ability that occasionally surfaced.

We played lots of games together. Jenga was one of my favourites. Once, I tipped all the blocks onto the table. She saw this and said there are hundreds of pieces to stack.

I looked at them and said, "No, there are only fifty-four."

She wasn't sure of this, so she counted them.

Amazed by my accuracy, she took out the KerPlunk game, counted the plastic straws then dropped them all onto the table and said, "How many?"

"Twenty-nine," I said.

My parents were told of this. Subsequently, I was assessed by the doctor. After going through the records of my developmental history and behaviour, they were told I had high functioning autism. They were concerned at first but they were put at ease by the in-depth explanation by our doctor.

Rehema often told my parents I was very bright for my age, although sometimes a bit too curious. I was always asking questions, wondering what things were and how they worked.

Mum's routine rarely changed, and I would always be at her side on market day when my siblings were at school or work. All market days were the same for me. First, we would browse the shoe stalls; Mum was always interested in fashion. After the family, shoes were her next love.

Because Dad was so successful, Mum now had the financial freedom to buy whatever took her fancy. She dressed well at all times; both her closets were full of beautiful clothes with something for all occasions, even her casual clothes were very smart but shoes she would have made and were always of her own design.

Mum always said carefully chosen footwear revealed a lot about a person. Although I never understood what she meant by that, I grew to love shoes too, and I always paid attention to people's footwear.

After looking at the shoes for inspiration, she would visit the meat stall to buy the halal lamb or whatever meat she needed for the next few days, then the vegetables and some fruit.

A chat to whatever friends she saw was also a part of market day. There was always a lot of chatting there.

Aged four and a half, I was stood next to Mum as she was chatting to her friends. Opposite, there was a stall selling small toy instruments made of wood and metal which I hadn't seen before or since. The stall holder caught my attention.

In an old style cap and dark glasses, he smiled. I don't know if he had something on his tooth, but it twinkled and at the same time, I heard a ping, like that of a triangle. As he smiled, he was doing some strange hand movements. He clicked his fingers on his right hand, then the same with his left, then he made it into a loose fist, and slapped it with the palm of his right hand, like he was slapping a sauce bottle. He was doing this a lot then drumming his fingers on the table in front of him. This intrigued me at the time, and I began to do it when I got home.

There were many feral animals in some of the areas Mum drove though on our way to the bazaar. With no one to care for them, many died of starvation and their rotting corpses were left to decompose in the heat. We would occasionally have a waft of this unpleasantness through the car vents. Whenever I smelt this or anything similar, it always reminded me of death.

Most of these animals were very cunning though. Many wandered the bazaar looking for scraps, sometimes stealing food when the trader's attention was elsewhere. I generally didn't pay them much attention. But as I was watching this man, he looked towards my feet and smiled again. I thought he liked my shoes.

I didn't notice it until I felt it brush around my leg. A very odd-looking unkempt cat began winding itself around my leg. In desperate need of care, there was beauty in this scrawny little thing with patchy matted fur.

Its eyes.

My attention focused on the oddity and vibrancy of them immediately.

One azure blue, the other blood red.

As I bent down to smooth it, it ran, then stopped to look back.

I walked towards it. I tried again and it did the same. It did this four times, I believed, in an attempt for me to follow. It led me a short distance through the market.

Being the largest of markets, I thought I shouldn't wander too far just in case I couldn't find my mother again. I continued looking back to check she was still in the same place.

Approaching a large doorway, I checked again. Mum was still there.

I turned to the cat. It had gone.

Before making my way back, I happened to glance into the doorway when I saw something shiny. My curiosity peaked so I investigated.

Getting closer, I could see it was some kind of ball and as I bent to pick it up it flickered with light. Blue and red, just like the cat's eyes.

I put it straight in my pocket and ran back to Mum.

She hadn't even noticed I had gone, and continued talking for a little while longer.

Once her friends left, she continued shopping and browsing, and once she had all the ingredients she needed, we made our way home.

On arrival, I hurried to my bedroom and hid the ball. If any of my siblings saw it, I knew they would take it for themselves.

We were never idle. Mum always kept us busy with something. We had our chores and Mum ensured Rehema knew to keep us busy, always.

Being the youngest, unfortunately I was always first to bed, but that night I was looking forward to it so I could explore my new found spherical gem.

Once retrieved from its hiding place, I could see the LEDs encapsulated, and part of the wheel exposed at the base, but on every turn, it emitted nothing. I wasn't even sure it was the wheel that caused the lights to flicker, but I tried to spin it faster anyway, running it across the floor with a quick sweep of my arm.

My arm would come to ache quickly each time, and after many weeks of this, I finally gave up, but still, I told no one of it.

I hid it again and eventually I forgot all about it.

We had our own rooms, so the house was larger than most. Initially a dilapidated shell, Dad bought it many years before for a price too small to pass. He and his brothers renovated it over a period of four years, and added some modern features, but mainly it went back to its original state, including bare block walls. It was a very old house and there were plenty of nooks, crannies and other obscure places where I could hide some of the things I didn't want anyone else to find and take from me. There were so many I couldn't remember them all, even back then.

When I found the ball again, I was six and a half years old. On reflection, I think it happened because Amelia and Claudia had just embarked on their first inter-dimensional adventure.

Whilst walking down the corridor to the kitchen, there was a vibrating noise coming from one of my many forgotten hiding places. It sounded like the vibration of a phone but it was ongoing. It took me a while, but I located the sound. It had been so long since I put it there, I had no idea what it could be. As I gently eased the loose block from the wall, I could see the blue and red flashing lights again. Excited by this, once again I took it to my room.

Being a little older, I was becoming more analytical in my thinking and as I sat on my bed, I began to study this mysterious thing.

Held upside down, there was an exposed part of the inner wheel and as I studied it, I noticed some small and not very deep holes within the groove encircling the centre. As before, I tried spinning the wheel with my hand, with no luck. Then I thought, *if I can wind a piece of string or something around the wheel, then pull, it should get it going.*

I hunted around the house for something that would do this and I came across an old pair of Dad's shoes. They looked expensive and the laces were of a fine material but I took one anyway. It fitted almost perfectly, but I did have to cut down the end a bit first, so it would fit snuggly in the hole.

I wound it on slowly and tightly, then pulled it as fast as I could.

It worked! The lights flashed intermittently. As I studied it, any slight movement from me produced a force, which felt strange. As I moved my hand more vigorously, the force became greater, the rotation grew faster and the lights became brighter. This ball was amazing!

It was strenuous on my wrist and arm, so I stopped and studied it further. It had a digital display with one button either side. The display read four ones. Unsure of what this represented, I pressed one of the buttons. It now read all zeros.

I re-wound the lace and pulled again. With an idea of what the digits may be, I tried to spin it faster.

When the muscle ache became too much, I stopped and checked the numbers.

It now displayed: 0314. I presumed it was a record of its revolutions per minute. I enjoyed playing with it, but it wasn't a toy I could play with continually as my wrist would ache after using it. I used it three or four times a week and within a month, I had mastered it.

One evening, Mum and Dad went out for dinner and, as usual, Rehema put me to bed at eight o'clock. I wasn't tired and couldn't sleep, so I began to search through my toys to see what I could play with. I came across my ball first, so I thought I would start with that while I was looking for something that interested me more. I loved educational toys and found my tablet which had lots of games loaded on it but I didn't fancy that. While I was thinking of what other things I had to play with, I didn't realise the ball was spinning faster and faster.

A golden wispy thread emerged from it and into my eye-line. There was a flash and, before I could think of stopping, my bedroom had disappeared and I was hurtling along a tube.

It was quite painful on my head because the resistance was pulling at my hair.

I'm sure it had some effect because it felt longer!

I was going so fast along this tube I wondered if it would ever stop. I had to close my eyes because it was like I was stood in front of a very powerful fan.

The resistance stopped and I opened my eyes. I was surrounded by a toy shop.

Stood in the entrance way, absorbing my environment, I was trying to figure out what just happened.

The sign above me read:

Welcome to

VIRTUE

All Reality Toys

Planet NEPENTHE'S Ultimate Adventure Destination

I was unsure of what was meant by "NEPENTHE", but I would ask Mum or Dad when I got back or look it up in the dictionary. I didn't know if it was a real planet as I'd never heard of it before.

I felt different, but I didn't know why and my concerns of how I ended up there soon faded as I looked around.

The store was the largest I had ever seen. There were so many different things, I didn't know where to go first. Everything observed so far in this store seemed to be electrical and digital, apart from the clock below the sign.

It looked like an old analogue railway clock. A large round brown casing, with an off-white dial, three ornate hands and no numbers. Instead, there were three words. "Now" was in the place of ten and two and at the bottom, the word "Present" replaced the six. The clock had only nine hours instead of twelve. This suggested wherever we were only had eighteen-hour days. Though it was odd, it didn't keep my attention for long and I continued my observations.

There were no signs or descriptions to indicate what the toys and items were, but I think that may have been to make people interact with them and figure them out for themselves.

The first thing that caught my eye was a stand with shelves full of shimmering electric blue boxes. From a distance, the boxes were arranged like they were balanced on one corner, but as I got closer, they were levitating about an inch off the shelf.

They weren't completely still as the bottom point of the box was slowly and gently making circular motions. Whilst trying to figure out how they were levitating, I noticed a girl walking towards the stand with both her arms stretched out in front of her.

She was about my height and I guess probably the same age too. She looked quite athletic, very slim, but solid, and she had shoulder-length dark brown hair.

She touched the stand and felt along the shelf. She realised what it was then started to feel what was on it. As her hands moved along the row of boxes, they began to spin, slowly at first, but I could see each one was gathering momentum. I don't think she could figure out what they were so she picked one up.

While she was feeling it all over, I heard her saying very quietly, "One box, six sides, and three prongs in a triangular shape on each side in the centre."

While she was engrossed in this box, the other boxes were still spinning. They looked beautiful, with the light dancing and jumping off the dark shimmering blue of the box.

Still gaining speed, they began to spark between the prongs, and the faster they went, the more the sparks looked like continuous gold circles surrounding the top and bottom halves of the box. These circles began to pulsate getting thicker and thinner, thicker and thinner until they met in the middle. All the boxes did this simultaneously and, as they reached that point, a thin wisp of smoky gold light emerged from the top of each box and began to spiral upwards in unison.

Once the light was almost at the ceiling, it went from a wispy light to a straight beam and there were thirty-seven light spots on the ceiling forming a square.

One by one, they gradually moved to the centre of the square, forming a tall slim pyramid shape.

The girl was oblivious to what was happening as she was still trying to figure out what she was holding.

The top point of the pyramid of golden light slowly began to lower until it reached the point where it began to look like a pyramid as I knew them. Once it reached that point, I thought how it looked like the Great Pyramid of Giza at home.

No sooner had I thought this, a beam of light shot from the point down to the box the girl was holding. When it hit the box, there was a crack and a flash. The surprise of which threw the girl onto her back, making her cry.

I rushed over and knelt by her side. As I wiped the tears from her eyes, she flinched. The shimmer that appeared around the tips of my fingers close to her eyes might have been why and I thought the light that knocked her off her feet might have caused that shimmer.

"Are you okay?" I asked as I wiped her eyes.

"Who are you?" she said.

"I'm Araminter."

"Where am I?"

"We're in a toy store."

"What, how did I get here? I was just in my bedroom."

Then it dawned on me. The last thing I remembered was I was in my bedroom too.

No one took any notice of what just happened; they carried on curiously with the items in the shop.

I helped her sit up and asked her name.

"Annie," she said as she put her hands out to feel me.

She started at my chest first, then moved up to my head then over my face, which freaked me out at first because there was something in her hand vibrating on my face. It was then I realised she was blind.

As she took her hand away from my face, I saw the ball.

I hadn't seen another one of these and I thought it was mine.

"Where did you get that?"

"What?" she said.

"That ball in your hand."

She held out her hands straight in front and slowly opened and closed them. She obviously couldn't feel it but as I watched her do this, I realised the ball was made of light. I could still see it as her fingers went in and out of it.

"What is the last thing you remember before you were here?" I asked.

"I was sat alone in my bedroom playing with my ball. I don't know what happened but my room sounded a lot bigger than it is, and there was a lot of noise from all these people. Something happened with a box I was holding and knocked me back to the floor, then you came over."

It seemed she had arrived the same way I did.

"Don't be upset," I said, "I have a ball like you, and exactly the same thing happened to me. But I don't know where mine is now; it must still be in my bedroom. Anyway, if we got here, we must be able to get back. Let's go outside and see if we can find out where we are."

I looked and looked but there were no doors or windows to the place, even what I thought was the entrance way had no door.

I stopped a man to ask where the exit was. He just laughed and walked away, which I thought was a bit rude.

Then I asked a lady, she said, "There is no way out, dear. No one ever leaves." And with a quizzical look on her face, she said, "Who are you with?"

As I looked around the store, there were no other children to be seen.

I quickly improvised.

"My parents, but I can't seem to find them."

"Well, you have all the time in the world, dear. You will find them eventually."

I thanked the lady, grabbed Annie's hand and headed towards an archway.

Annie stood watching people as they wandered through the store and said, "I'm not completely blind, you know. I can see light and outlines of things."

While we were looking around the store, a woman's voice came over a PA system. It was attempting to entice customers to enter something called the Themuru VANTABLACK Machine.

I had always been envious of how quickly others learnt and understood things as my extra chromosome did affect my learning, but then I realised why I felt different there. I was understanding things far quicker than normal.

I listened again. Intently this time.

"Do you want to be a better you? Do you want to eliminate all your negative thoughts? Join us in VANTABLACK and let us relieve you of the thoughts that hold you back. Your experience will be like no other. You don't even have to try. Everything is automatic.

"VANTABLACK will release you from your negativity and leave a more positive you. Venturing the depths of your mind, giving a greater understanding of your being. In your alternate realities you will see the u n seen, obtain c larity and see see seemore of the desires you hold. Become the participant and the o b servir. It's the only way to become."

Apart from the stutter, short pauses and the way she said "observer" in the recording, it sounded quite enticing, so I asked a lady at one of the many help desks where this VANTABLACK was.

Very pleasant but robotic in her manner, she pointed us in the right direction.

We continued to wander through the store, attempting to follow the directions. I held Annie's hand so people would know we were together and hopefully not stop and question us.

We seemed to be looking for a long time. We walked and walked, up the escalators, down the escalators, through long wide corridors, tall doorways, small doorways, trying out any toys that took our interest as we passed.

We turned a corner and saw the entrance to a room. The size of the pillars caught my attention.

With no windows to distract my focus, my gaze followed their smooth hard lines to the top. Confronted by a high-domed glass ceiling, the intense multi-coloured rays of light caused us to squint.

I said to a man who was passing, "What's causing all these colours?"

"Why do you ask?"

"Just curious. Is there anything above that glass ceiling?"

"Many great things happen on the other side, but it is unlikely that you will ever get to experience life above it. Only a few women have."

It was an odd response, and I didn't really understand what he meant at the time, but the implication was of being trapped below never to find a way out.

As we entered, the room was large, circular and very ornate. The prism-like panes of glass in the domed ceiling were arranged in such a way that the split light shone directly below onto each of the seven intricately carved marble pillars.

As my gaze lowered, the centre of the room held a monstrous machine. In comparison to what we saw up until that point, it looked very industrial and out of place. As if it belonged in a breaker's yard.

This was it and not at all what I expected.

In contrast to the beautifully coloured pillars, the name emblazoned on the machine was:

THEMURU

"VANTABLACK"

As the light hit the highly polished angled facets half way down each pillar, it created a rainbow-like band of coloured light encircling the machine. My surroundings had a certain serenity about them and I became entranced for a moment. Taking it all in, I was overcome by a dominating divine masculine energy.

Feeling no movement whilst holding my hand, Annie shook me out of my trance.

Appearing to be made up of many smaller parts, the bulk was round and metallic, topped with a large dome-shaped tank containing what looked like black eels. I assumed it was full of water because of the eels, but it was so clear they could have been floating. The longer I stared, the blacker they became eventually becoming two dimensional.

From the top of the dome, there was a large diameter trunk consisting of many different size pipes which arched overhead and connected to the surrounding six seating pods.

At the base of the machine in front of each pod, coupled together, were a number of sturdy but flexible thick wires or they could have been pipes. Interconnected, they threaded their way around the machine once, before they too suspended and arched themselves to connect with the pods.

Capacities were various: one single seater, a two-seater, two three-seaters, a four and a five. One of the partitions in the pod of four was full of, what I once again assumed to be, water.

It was being agitated vigorously and occasionally bits of debris would stick to the glass canopy. After a while, the water stopped moving and it drained through the base. There was a whistling sound that started high then very quickly adopted a low tone, followed by a continuous sound of air being forcibly blown. It came from one of the four large adjustable vents in the glass canopy that encased the seats. The air was hot and drying the pod. It steamed up very quickly.

The vents opened and I felt the release of the moist air, with a hint of death, blowing through my hair whilst peering in.

When the glass cleared, I noticed the three other people in the adjoined seats.

Sat motionless with the occasional twitch, they were dressed similar to fighter pilots. A dull khaki green jumpsuit and a helmet adorned with the essential paraphernalia.

What disturbed me was the sight of them being manacled.

Now paying more attention to the empty pod, I noticed the seat had two holes in the base.

The outer arched pipe pierced the canopy with a thinner black pipe protruding. It held the helmet and hanging from the inner visor were two tubes terminating with suckers. I described it to Annie and asked if she wanted to try this machine.

"What does it do?" she asked.

I told her I didn't know.

She then said, "I don't think there's much point. I won't be able to see anything anyway."

Deciding whether or not to get in, we heard a whistling noise.

We turned. A canopy began to raise on our right. With a hiss and a crackle of static, the contained pressure was released.

A large woman stepped out from the pod. With a beaming smile on her face, she looked approachable.

I asked her about the machine.

"It's a virtual life machine, dear," she said still holding the smile. "There's one on each of the six floors below us. The Root Cathedral Room VL in the basement is quite basic, but the experiences become deeper and more meaningful the closer you get to this one: The Crown Cathedral Room VL.

"I have tried them all, and though they are interconnected, this one is by far the best and most beneficial. It's why most of us come here."

She went on to explain further.

"The helmet's internal electrodes read your brain activity and analyse thought. The two tubes from the visor have suckers, which attach to your eyes. It's not so bad putting them on but you have to be careful when you take them off. People are known to have pulled their eyes from their sockets before now.

"As you put the mask on, the tubes retract a little as the sensors measure your mouth. It releases a small amount of anaesthetic lubricating fluid then gently extends tubes into your stomach. It can be a little uncomfortable when they're removed, but well worth it. Then you just hang on for the time of your life."

It sounded straightforward, but she omitted two points. Both quite important.

One of which was this machine wasted nothing.

Within the dome, the eels' faeces, dead eels and all impurities in the water were filtered out, blended, compressed into tiny pellets and fed through the pipe that entered the stomachs of all that chose to partake.

"Did you want to do it together?" the lady asked.

I looked at Annie and she agreed, although I felt there was some reluctance in her voice.

"You'll have to wait for a double pod, although you could go into a triple pod but then there's the possibility of someone joining you and when that happens, they become part of your VL."

I looked at her questioningly.

"Virtual life, dear."

After listening intently to the lady's description, it made us all the more curious, so we settled on a triple because we didn't want to wait.

I stepped inside as she noticed our attire was incorrect.

"Oh, you need jumpsuits, dear. Without it, the smell would get very bad indeed, unbearable even and may wake you."

She pointed to one of the archways. Above it, the sign read: Attirical Adornment.

We entered the changing room. At the time, I was unsure why we had to be naked but we were asked to remove all our clothes.

In the area of my bottom, and set into the suit, was what I can only describe as a large cupped knee pad with two connections on the outside at the bottom. It did feel odd at first but when we returned to the machine and sat, it fitted like a glove.

Realising we were alone, the lady asked, "Where are your parents?"

"Oh, we're meeting them later," I quickly replied, and thankfully, she accepted this.

"Would you like some help setting up?"

We accepted her offer

I went on to ask, "My friend is almost blind, so does she have to put the suckers on her eyes?"

"Blind?" she said with a smile. "Oh yes, most definitely! If she is blind, she will have the most amazing experience."

It all sounded a bit odd, but we went along with it.

Annie's spirits seemed to lift a little and I could see she was becoming more excited. Annie sat down first and as she settled into the seat, she pointed.

"What's that flickering light?"

She was pointing to the large dome on top of the machine.

Shortly after the pod I was previously watching had dried, the dome had a simultaneous influx and extraction of fluid.

Without warning, the eels went into a frenzy. This sight was mesmerising and, on reflection, it was more of a seductive almost choreographed dance of chaotic orderliness.

The beams of light selected gaps between the blackness and shone with a rapid flicker onto Annie's face only. She did look beautiful.

I later learnt what "VANTABLACK" meant.

The lady continued to tell us of the machine and why it was so popular.

"Most of the people that use this machine want to become better people by removing their negativity and, through the electrodes, your negative thoughts slowly seep from your mind to the water and that is what the eels feed off. Though transparent at birth, like a clear jelly, they get blacker the more they feed, and with the amount of people that use this machine, there is an endless supply of nutrition for the eels."

The lady leant in and placed the helmet on Annie's head. She extracted the suckers from the visor and slowly aligned them to the centre of her eyes.

"This may feel a bit uncomfortable. They will tug on your eyes a little, until the suction has no leaks."

Annie was uncomfortable with the thought of this and asked if I would hold her hand. I obliged.

A vacuum tube removed some air from the mask and sealed itself on her face. As it reached equilibrium, it released an incapacitating agent. In a moment, consciousness left her body. She went limp and my hand dropped from hers.

I looked at the lady in panic.

"Oh, it's all right, dear. That's normal. It shows that everything is working as it should."

As I looked at the others hooked up to this machine, and apart from the occasional twitch, I could see there was no movement; they were all limp in their seats.

She explained the process as another tube discharged anaesthetic lubricant and inched its way down her throat.

"Your brain activity is monitored throughout and you remain unconscious until your VL ends," she told me.

I stepped in and sat back in the chair ready for the hook up.

With the bubbling excitement, along with the nervousness, in the back of my mind was the thought of my ball and how myself and Annie actually got here.

Then, darkness.

I opened my eyes. Still in the toy store, I was unsure if this was what alternate reality was.

I looked around. There were many statues of clowns, which I hadn't noticed previously. They may have been there, but I was so engrossed in everything around me and the spectacle of the machine, maybe I hadn't noticed.

Another child's voice called my name. I had seen no other children in the store and I didn't tell anyone else my name so I knew it was Annie. I turned to see her coming down the escalator. She was smiling and waving at me, carrying a bag ready to burst at the seams. She reached the bottom of the escalator and ran over.

"This is amazing! I can see everything!" She grabbed my hand and dragged me. "I've been looking everywhere for you. Where have you been? Never mind, come on. Let's explore!"

Joseph

After the lightning strike, Joseph was never the same. He hadn't been able to hold down a job since the hospital. The power of the bolt changed his bio-electrical circuitry and the blinding flash made him very sensitive to light.

He endured regular blackouts, sometimes for days on end, and found it difficult to function in society. When the blackouts first started, he became very confused with reality. After what happened, everyone who knew him became concerned for his wellbeing. It had been over six years since the storm and there had been very little improvement in his self-care.

Over the years, his visitors grew less and less and very little crossed his threshold including himself.

The energy of his house gradually seeped away taking the kerb appeal with it. Dirty windows, crumbling bricks and a splintered door gained it the reputation of the haunted house of the area. The façade was now looking old.

Everybody local to the area knew what had happened to him at the time of the storm and his shunning of the media during the aftermath caused much speculation about him.

He hadn't had a single visitor in the last year and was only ever seen as a glancing shadow at the window. This is what started rumours and stories amongst local teenagers.

They would tell the younger children, "When you pass his house, don't look in, because you won't see anything. But if he's near the window, and he notices you, you'll only see the glowing of his eyes in the darkness behind the nets.

"He's always there, watching, and when he sees a child he wants to abduct, his eyes glow deep purple and when eye contact is made, you become frozen to the spot.

"Then, in a long dark cloak, he rushes out and grabs you. He's aware of who's around, and children always go missing when they're alone and no one else is on the street. No one has ever seen him do it and there has only been one child to escape from their imprisonment in his house, and that's how we know about him."

As this story spread throughout the children in the community, they were reluctant to walk past the house and if they had to, they would either run or cross the road, not giving it a single look.

The parents, though aware of the rumour, knew it was exactly that, and even though immediate neighbours would occasionally knock to see if he was okay, their attempts to help were never met.

Seven years to the day, early evening, there was a knock on his door.

He went to the bay window to see who was there prior to answering. The shock of who he saw made him stumble backwards, tripping over his chair and banging his head on the solid oak occasional table.

This time, he blacked out for three days.

Annie

The circumstances were similar, but there was a traumatic aspect to my birth.

My body had formed perfectly, my brain wired correctly with all neural pathways and synapses ready for moulding to make me the person I wanted to be. My environment was purely sensory.

I could feel, taste and hear. I knew all nerve endings for my nose were wired in the right places, and that my sense of smell would work because it had connections to my tongue and sense of taste, but my sight was another matter. I wasn't sure about my eyes.

I connected all the necessary neural pathways for sight but I couldn't be a hundred percent sure. Every time I opened my eyes, there was always darkness. The opportunity to experiment as I did with my other senses wouldn't arise until my birth.

The eternal darkness kept me constant in my work to get some kind of result.

Nothing!

Darkness persisted.

In my peaceful surroundings, I should have been resting after what I had created, but the last moments in my mother's womb were consumed with doubt. Time was running out.

The gradual solidification of DNA material that encapsulated my consciousness was almost complete. Innately, I knew it had to be sealed in prior to birth.

I could have aborted anytime up until the complete encapsulation, but after all I had achieved, I continued till the last.

I believed, once the consciousness was sealed in, I was ready. Unaware I was so far ahead of schedule, I activated enzymes and proteins and created more amniotic fluid to be sure.

Forced from, what I call, my comfortable place at twenty-six weeks, my head emerged and instinctively I attempted my first breath.

The oxygen supply from my mother ceased due to the umbilical cord around my neck and the midwife did all she could to remove it without causing me trauma. Eventually, they succeeded.

Apart from the fact I was fourteen weeks early and worryingly underweight, everything else was as expected, including the occasional power outages caused by the storm.

I was kept in an incubator for another two and a half months. The day Mum and Dad had waited so long for arrived and I was taken home.

They took great care of me, but after a while they had some concerns about my sight.

I recently asked Mum what alerted her to my blindness. She told me that, during the first four months, she noticed my eyes weren't moving normally. At first, she assumed it was because I was a newborn, but she grew more concerned as time passed and booked a paediatric assessment at six months.

The results were far worse than Mum and Dad expected. They were told I was almost completely blind, most likely caused by a premature birth and oxygen starvation.

The devastation caused didn't negatively affect my upbringing, it enhanced it, and unless it was impossible because of my blindness, I was treated exactly the same as my brother Michael.

In the beginning, it was difficult for them all, but to me, I knew no different. As far as I was concerned, I was normal and often wondered why they fussed so much. Not wanting the fuss that came from their love, I grew to be very independent.

I loved my brother dearly and we did almost everything together; he was like my guide. It was hard for me to make friends because of my limited sight, but Michael, even though he was younger than me, always pushed me to break the boundaries I believed I had.

When we played outside, he would clear a path the full length of the garden and make me race him. He told me it was a straight run with no obstacles. We stood with our backs against the wall of the house and I waited for him to say go.

Because of the visual impairment, my hearing was acute, so my spatial awareness was pretty good.

"Ready, steady, go!"

As soon as he said go, we both pushed ourselves off the wall and ran as fast as we could. I was so focused on winning I was always listening to where he was, and as it was our first race, he didn't tell me to stop when we got to the end of the garden, and within the split second I realised how close I was, it was too late.

I was reluctant to do it after the first time because I almost broke my nose, but he did convince me to do it again.

There were a few minor accidents in most of the things he got me to do, but it was worth it, and being the only two children, doing all of those things together was what made us so close.

Very few of our toys were gender specific and we would play with anything from empty boxes to the electronic toys available to us, including Michael's collection of clowns. He loved his clowns and had been collecting them for as long as I could remember. Pockets was his first and had always been his most cherished. He was so named because his costume was made entirely of pockets.

Toys weren't allowed in the bedroom. We were always told bedrooms were for sleeping, so the spare room became the place for all of our things. A wise choice by our parents; this kept our bedrooms relatively tidy.

Along with all my things, I thought I knew of everything Michael owned.

It was a late Saturday afternoon and I was feeling bored. Michael was out with Dad, and Mum was cooking, so I went to the playroom.

I was looking for such a long time I was almost ready to go help Mum with the baking.

With my hands deep in one of the boxes rummaging amongst the hard and soft, I came across something curious. It felt like a hard ball.

With a flat base and part of what felt like a wheel protruding, it wasn't completely spherical. Unable to recall this item, I removed it from amongst the other toys and felt it properly. Running my fingers over every surface, there was something that felt like it shouldn't be part of this ball. Where the ball was hard and cold, this felt soft and a bit warmer. It was very small and felt like material.

I held the ball close to my eyes, hoping it was more than an outline I could see.

The ball itself was transparent. The material, a vibrant red, wasn't stuck to the ball, so I began to ease it out.

I thought it was a shoelace at first as it had the plastic aglet around one end; the other was missing and the thin string frayed.

I put it to one side and continued to study and feel the ball. There was a distinctive top and bottom to it. It was hard plastic with an opening at the bottom. The top was flat and mainly smooth with two buttons. Internally was a hard cold wheel.

As I turned the wheel with one finger, I held my thumb over the flat edge. There was a groove all the way around it and I felt small holes evenly spaced within. The wheel spun freely, so I held the ball in one hand and ran it over the palm of my other hand trying to make the wheel spin. After many attempts, the wheel would stop as quickly as I got it started. I was just about to give up, when I remembered I already had something similar to this.

My gyroscope.

That needed a string to start it.

I picked up the string I removed earlier and placed the plastic-bound end into one of the tiny holes in the wheel. I slowly turned the wheel and wound it almost fully.

Sat snug in the groove with enough left for me to get a firm hold, I pulled the string as fast as I could. It emitted a flickering light. I held it in my hand as it spun and flashed. Although it was different to my gyroscope, I was expecting a bit more than what I saw. Bored of it already, I went to put it down, but as I did, there was a definite force until I held it still again. I brought it back up and the force returned.

At least it does something, I thought, and I tried to do this quicker. As I did, it had a definite vibration like it was about to fall apart, but as soon as I stopped moving it up and down, the vibration stopped, even though the wheel was still spinning.

I continued again but at a slower pace. To my amazement, the ball began to spin faster. Rarely did I find toys that accentuated my senses.

The subtle sensation from the exerting force, the visual stimulus of the lights growing brighter and the faint sound as the pitch grew higher the faster it spun excited three of my five senses.

Though it was fun, it was very strenuous and I had to stop for a while to rest my arm and wrist before going again. Moving my hand up and down quickly gave it momentum, then as I slowed my wrist action, the internal wheel's speed increased and something changed.

Everything was different.

My toy room was far bigger than a moment ago and there were a lot of people around me.

Being quite independent, there wasn't much that bothered me, especially if I was with Mum, Dad or Michael, but when I worried about anything, the six tiny moles on my temple would gently pulsate.

This was one of those times. Something was very wrong.

As I got up, I realised I didn't have my stick.

I had to know where I was, so with my arms out I slowly made my way forward, trying to find something that would hopefully give me some idea of where I was and what had happened.

Slowly making my way forward, and trying to figure out where I was, I came to something which felt like a shelving unit. Slowly feeling my way along, there were quite a few things on the shelf, so I picked one up to find out what it was.

Feeling a box with something rattling inside, I felt three prongs on all sides. My fingers became rigid as I sensed a mild electrical energy. With my minimal sight focused on the box, I was intent on figuring out what it was I was holding, all the while oblivious to everything else around me.

The closer I brought it to my eyes, the smaller it became, and the electrical energy increased.

A shock surged through me, tensing my muscles and with no control over my body, I fell backwards knocking myself unconscious for a while.

The hand holding the box remained tense and I couldn't open it for quite a while afterwards. Consequently, it was still in my hands when we saw the VL machine, and with my attention now on the machine, my hand began to relax and I released my grip to put it in my pocket.

Though extremely scared at first, another girl came to my aid. Her name was Araminter. She was really nice to me. She helped me up, calmed me down and explained where we were. But as I had no idea how I got there, I was still worried I wouldn't get back home.

She took me around the shop and described lots of things to me. We heard a voice over the Tannoy and Araminter asked someone where VANTABLACK was.

As we continued walking, the acoustics changed. It now sounded like a cathedral type room, and there was something in the middle of the room that Araminter was very curious about.

She began to talk to someone about this thing in the room. She was asking a lady about something with lots of pipes on it. My mind was still on getting home, then I heard the lady say, "Blind? Oh yes, most definitely! If she is blind, she will have the most amazing experience."

And when Araminter asked me if I wanted to go on it, I immediately said, "Yes."

Once we had the correct attire, Araminter helped me into the pod, and the lady proceeded to fit my helmet. She began to lift my eyelids and place the suckers on to my eyeballs. They were very uncomfortable.

Once attached, the mask sucked itself onto my face and released a pipe which edged its way down my throat. It made me cough, then everything went black.

I opened my eyes.

Wow!

With no additional adornment and clothes I had never seen before, it was awesome. I could see everything.

Wonderful as it was, I did feel a little uneasy for a while. Though I could see perfectly, I sensed I was being watched. There was something unusual about this. I wondered if this was how "seeing people" felt, being watched because they could watch. I looked around and saw no one looking at me and assumed that was the case, so I began to explore.

I was so excited, I forgot about Araminter for a while and I went wandering around the store.

There were so many things I'd never felt or seen before. I picked up a bag and began to fill it with all that took my fancy. Being a kid in a sweet shop had nothing on this. A kid in a toy shop was so much better!

As the bag was getting almost too heavy to carry, I remembered Araminter and thought I should look for her. Worry began to set in. It took me longer than expected, but from the top of the escalator, I spotted her. I shouted to get her attention.

She saw me and ran over. I grabbed her hand, told her I could see everything and dragged her through the store.

Carrying the bag was getting uncomfortable, so I left it in a doorway to collect later.

It felt like we were there forever, trying to explore every floor, but there didn't seem to be any end to the mysterious store. There was something that wasn't quite right though.

What Araminter hadn't mentioned earlier were the number of clowns in the store. I noticed them immediately. They reminded me of Michael. I had played with his clowns a lot when I was younger, and the thing about these was they looked exactly the same as Michael's clowns had felt to me. They reminded me of my brother, so I was comfortable with them and thought nothing more of it.

Araminter

I had the most wonderful time with my new friend Annie. Exploring this shop with all these toys was amazing, but at the same time, it was tiring. I told her we should think about getting out of this machine and then try to figure out how to get back home.

She laughed and said, "I forgot we were in a machine. How do we get out?"

Then it dawned on me; I hadn't asked the lady how to get out, so I thought I had better ask someone.

We turned a corner and saw a door. We headed for it almost breaking out into a run, thinking as well as a way out of the shop it would be the way out of this reality. As soon as we got outside, we stopped in our tracks. It was a sight I couldn't have dreamt of.

It was a rainbow sky. Not a sky full of rainbows, but a densely clouded multi-coloured sky but it wasn't dull. The light streamed through the clouds' vivid colours. Description is difficult, because most of the colours I had never seen before.

The breaks in the density of the cloud revealed two moons: one blue and one red. They looked so close I felt I could have touched them with my fingertips.

We both stood in awe, consumed by the moment.

While Annie was still taking it in, I began to look around to see who we could ask. Though we thought we were outside, we had no idea in which direction to go. Not that it would make any difference.

We were cold and, still thinking of how to get out of here, I rubbed my hands together to warm them a little. They warmed surprisingly quickly and, as I looked at them, they had that same shimmer I saw on my fingertips when I wiped Annie's tears away, but I was unsure if there was any connection to the first beam of light that appeared to cause it or the light streaming through the clouds.

Uneasy, we wandered for a while, eventually getting a sense of being followed. However, every time we looked back, nobody looked suspicious.

We approached a number of people, and asked the same question.

"How do we get out of this reality?"

The problem we had was the majority of people we asked must have been hooked up for so long, they had no idea what we were talking about. Nothing we said triggered the memory of VANTABLACK. They had forgotten their origin and were living the only reality they knew. They looked at us as if we were mad.

On hearing our question, one man laughed at us.

Another said, "You don't really want to know how you get out of this reality."

Then another, with deep furrows in his brow and a loud scary voice, said, "Death!"

A bit upset by his manner, we thought we would find a nice lady to ask, which we did, but she answered us with a question.

"Why do you want to know?"

We explained, and even though I don't think she believed us, we could see it triggered something within her.

She took a while to answer. Brows narrowed and glazed eyes, she had a searching look on her face as if she was trying to recall a deeply buried long dead memory.

She did answer our question eventually, but her answer, although told in a kinder way, was the same as what the previous man had told us.

Then I remembered. The lady that helped us into the machine said, "Once it takes over your brain, you become unconscious until your VL ends." But she never said how to regain consciousness and end the virtual life.

As the nice lady left, we continued walking. We were discussing scenarios of what may happen if we could never get out of this reality, then Annie said, "Can you hear that?"

We stopped and listened. Annie's hearing was far more acute than mine.

"Argh! That's really loud. It's hurting my ears."

Then I heard the whistling noise, gradually getting louder. Then there was the sound of a whoosh of air then a loud static crackle.

"What was that?" I asked Annie.

She had no idea, so we carried on walking. But as we both looked ahead, in the distance, we saw a clown coming towards us. He didn't seem to be exerting any effort and there was no sign of body movement in his approach. He got closer and we noticed he was floating.

This rattled us a bit, so we turned and ran as fast as we could, but being children, the clown, without effort, caught us almost immediately.

Thinking of the number of clowns in the toy shop, I wondered whether VANTABLACK had misinterpreted our brainwaves and we had subconsciously created them. Either that or, as the lady that helped us into the machine said, someone had taken the empty seat in our pod and it was he or she chasing us.

The clown caught us. He held out both arms and picked us up with ease. We screamed as loud as we could, trying to get the attention of other people on the street, but as we looked, there was no one. The once semi-bustling street was now deserted.

Amidst our screaming and crying, I heard him say, "It's okay. I'm not going to hurt you. I'm only here to help you. I'm the one you've been looking for. I've been waiting an eternity for you and I'm here only to get you out of this world.

"You can ask as many people as you want, but I am the only one here willing to help and if you want to get out, you have to trust me."

We calmed ourselves just enough for his words to sink in. Annie and I looked at each other and with no other option, we listened.

We were unsure of his motives and he knew he would have to trick us into doing what he said in order to get us back to the original toy shop.

He took us to a place which I think may have been his home and, on arrival, I thought he was going to put us in a car and take us somewhere to get us out of this place, but when I asked about his car, he had no idea what I was talking about.

When I tried to explain what a car was, he looked at me as if I was making it up. I thought he was going to say he travels by some kind of flying machine, but he said, "That sounds painfully slow. No, we travel by a far quicker method. It's the Digital Expulsion And Time Hyperactivity 2 Unit."

We should have known, but I was never that good at recognising acronyms in speech.

He took us into the place he lived. I would say house but I'd never seen one like it before. It looked more like a grounded UFO.

On approach, a door raised automatically and we climbed the now visible staircase and once over the threshold, it closed behind us. We walked along a few corridors passing a number of rooms. The door was open to one of the rooms we passed and in two of the recesses, there were holograms of a woman. I didn't take it all in immediately but as we continued, I realised it was the woman who had helped us into the machine. We reached the room and he asked Annie for the box. I had no idea what he was talking about when she produced the prong-sided box.

With opposite corners held between his finger and thumb, he gently blew. Accompanied with an incantation repeated three times, the box opened like a flower exposing three rings.

He told us to take for ourselves the ring we felt most attracted to.

Once chosen, he told us what they were and the symbolic properties they held, although he didn't need to tell me what my choice of ring was. I have always loved diamonds.

He took us to the room where the unit was and explained how it worked.

Annie chose the lapis lazuli ring which symbolised strength and courage whereas mine symbolised strength, love and health.

The remaining ring had two stones: one of fluorite crystal and the other of opal. Apart from the rainbow of colours, it had transformational properties, boosted mental clarity and promoted peace of mind.

The description of the final ring made me want to change my mind, but as I tried to swap them, the clown closed his hand and said, "No," continuing to tell us the importance of resonance.

Once he'd finished, he told us to sit and wait.

Before he closed the door, he said the room would fill with steam and we would soon be back at the original toy store.

If we did actually die in that room, it wasn't bad at all. It was like falling asleep in one place and waking in another.

When we regained consciousness, the pipe automatically retracted from our throats, air was pumped into our masks to release from our faces and we both removed our helmets.

We looked at each other and laughed nervously, and as I looked at the seat next to me, it was empty so the clown didn't come from here as I thought.

The worst part of the whole thing wasn't the clown, but getting those suckers off my eyes. It was far more painful than we were first told.

Now we were out of the virtual life machine, we needed to get back to our own reality, and the only way I could think of was by using the spheres we both had.

Because we couldn't see or feel our own, we would have to start each other's, and even though Annie was almost blind once again, I knew she would be able to start mine. All we had to do was find some string to get the balls started.

I looked for a long time to find something that would work, but there was nothing, no manual toys, not even gyroscopes. Then I had an idea.

Though shoes are one of the first things I notice about people, all the time I was here I never glanced at them at all. It was probably because there were far more interesting things around. Then, appearing in front of me was a golden rat. I observed it scurrying around people's feet.

I looked at the people passing us and the people stood around; not one of them had any footwear with laces. I didn't think any of the women would have had them, but I expected to see at least one pair of lace ups on a man. I found it unusual that they were all slip-on shoes or Velcro uppers.

The rat was scurrying around, circling me in a spiral in and out of sight as if to attract my attention. Having seen no other vermin, I took Annie's hand and decided to follow it.

Losing sight of the rat at times, we were heading back to the VL machine. I was really hoping I could find someone with what I needed.

I told Annie to stay put as I went in search of someone with laces in their shoes. In the single and double pods were women and they all had strappy shoes. Then, through the corner of my eye, I noticed something moving through the air. I turned and saw the rat heading straight for the canopy of the pod of four. Expecting it to crash into the glass and slide down the curve, to my amazement, it went straight through.

I went over and peered in. There was no sign of it, but as I looked through the glass cover, the third man in the row had a pair of shoes just like my father: the same design and the same fine laces. I pressed the button and lifted the catch and as I began to prize open the lid, there was a whistling sound then a whoosh of air and finally a static discharge. As soon as these three things happened, I remembered the clown.

He appeared in our alternate reality moments after I heard those very sounds. Though unsure, I dismissed it at the time. I was now convinced he took the last seat in our pod. Did he know something? Was he only there to rescue us or was he really a child killer?

Anyway, the main thing was we were back.

There wasn't much room in the pod. All seats were taken but I managed to get over to the far side to the man with the laces. I managed to get the lace from the shoe, left the pod and closed it. The plastic aglets were very short, which was a good thing as we didn't have any way of shortening them.

I returned to Annie, placed the aglet into the wheel of her ball, wound on the lace and pulled.

It worked.

I placed the lace in her hand and asked her to do the same to mine. It took a little longer because she had to feel for the hole but she managed to get it going because as soon as the string was pulled, I moved my hand and felt the force from the ball.

We kept the ball going slowly while we said our goodbyes.

We sped up the balls, then… darkness.

Back in my room, my inner feeling was electric. Ball in hand, I stood at my window staring as my imagination dreamt up all kinds of adventures, but my trance was broken by a thud as the ball fell from my hands.

The heavy impact resulted in the release of gold vapours, many more than the usual solitary wisp. Changing colour as they circled the ball, it looked like an ever-expanding aura. The rapid change of colour eventually became white before shooting away.

Though separate, the core of the balls originated from the same tektite quasar and, as a consequence, they are eternally connected and attracting each other.

So strong was the attraction emitting from the microscopic fracture on their release from the surrounding gravitational field, initially the white light instantaneously headed in the direction of the nearest of the other six balls.

Only to swerve off course.

The attraction of two balls together is four-fold, increasing exponentially with each additional ball until the seven become one. So, even though Phreya's was closer, it was Amelia and Claudia that benefitted from this accidental release of power.

The location of the balls in their bedroom turned out to be crucial. The wispy vapours, now a dense ball of light, travelled from day to night across five or six time zones.

Only able to guess its identity and origin, it was described as a vision of the iconic electric light orchestra spaceship. The red and blue entity constant in its glow delighted those lucky enough to witness it.

Following the trajectory of a shallow arc, it reached its destination.

Completely missing the open window, it shuddered the house to its foundations as it passed through the wall.

Quickly decreasing in size, it encased Amelia, Claudia and both balls for a moment and left remnants of the knowledge-imbued light with them.

Phreya

When we left the ethers, we were so excited in anticipation of our creation and the lives ahead of us. As a group and as individual consciousness, we sensed the vibrational variety of all we could be as creators.

From the beginning, it was excited anticipation of what could be and as pure consciousness with no resistance, our focus was sharper than any could imagine.

However, once the journey of creation began, we realised there was no way of knowing who as a person or where in the world each of us would end up.

We had to put our trust in ourselves and belief in our source to ensure we recognised our instinctive urges to find each other once again.

Once physical beings, of the seven, I probably had the most resistance as I was not what I expected myself to be. As far as I knew, I was the same as any other child and life was normal, until the day I became gender aware.

I had that inexplicable feeling. Instinctively, I knew something wasn't right and realising the error in my creation, I was absolutely mortified.

My happiness waned and from that day forward, I couldn't bear anything that suggested I was feminine. I was determined to be a boy. It wasn't anything I believed I had control over, I just knew I wasn't right and I had to live my life in the most comfortable way for me, regardless of what anyone else thought or did.

Mum and Dad knew there was something different because I began to ask a lot of questions about the differences of being a boy and being a girl, and when I could become a boy.

Surprised at my questions, they answered as best they could, but not to my satisfaction. I was their only child and my happiness was as important to them as it was to me.

Understanding my plight at such a young age, they would buy boys' shoes and clothes for me, and let me have a boy's haircut, but even though they did all they could, it never changed my feelings or what I thought was the impossible.

I grew distant from those that didn't understand me because they mocked me for my choices and I eventually became a loner.

When Mum and Dad were at work, I was dropped off at day care, but thankfully Mum worked part-time, so I was only there three days a week. Whilst there, I rarely interacted with anyone. I never felt comfortable with the girls because I knew I was mentally different to them and I wasn't interested in anything girly, and I didn't want to play with the boys because they always treated me like a girl.

I had no one.

The first year of infant school was the worst I have ever had to endure. All staff were made aware of my situation, and even after dressing me in boy's clothes as I had insisted, my mother was still approached by parents and even some teachers to find out why she was doing this to me. Consequently, my pastoral care was discussed as part of the agenda at the governors' meeting, and because of the pressures of political correctness, equality and our rights as children in their care, in their wisdom they decided to tell the whole class about how I was different and how I should be treated by them.

As a result of this, I ended up an outcast.

No one understood me and it was very hard to cope with. I needed an escape.

The only time I wasn't sad was when I was alone, and the only time I was anything even close to being happy was when I was alone amongst nature. I think the plants benefitted from that too. I always talked to them.

My parents knew why I was sad all the time, but to put it right for me was physically out of their control. Occasionally they would buy me something just to cheer my mood a little because they suffered some emotional distress too.

They knew I was happiest when I was amongst nature, so for my sixth birthday they took me to the gardens at Glansevern Hall. With the River Severn nearby, it was a fantastic place and very special to me. There was such a variety of trees, flowers and plants, also a lake and a pond with a fountain, but what excited me most was the walled garden. It sounded mysterious. Unfortunately, the day we went, the walled garden was closed, but I went to the large wooden door anyway.

There was a small hole where a knot in the wood had fallen out. I tried to peer through when my palm began to itch. I scratched it excessively; it felt like it would never stop. Eventually, I looked to see what was causing it. To my surprise, there was an imprint of a circle with a plus sign, an arrow and a combination of the two coming out of it. I didn't tell Mum or Dad about it because as soon as I saw what it was, it disappeared.

There was very little visible through the small hole, which was disappointing, but that added another dimension to it and I knew I had to return there someday.

We didn't always have to travel that far to appreciate nature as there were many places close to where we lived. One of my favourites was Castell Coch or the Red Castle. We were told the tooth fairies lived there. I believed it because it looked exactly as I imagined a fairy castle to be, and being in the middle of a forest added an air of mystery to it.

Still quite happy as I thought of my birthday outing, my sadness came back once I returned to school the following Monday.

I continued to suffer the jokes and insults from many of the other pupils and this continued until June arrived. I was so looking forward to the summer holidays, no more insults and lewd remarks for at least six weeks. It was this thought that kept me going.

The weather was unusually warm for the end of June as our summers of the past didn't start until mid or late July.

When Mum and Dad picked me up on the last day of school, they could see my sadness had lifted. Walking to the gates with a smile on my face, they assumed I'd had a good day. I was happier and that day we went to the city to buy Dad new shoes for work.

On leaving the car park on the way to the shops, I noticed there were a lot of scruffy people sat near shop doorways begging. I turned to Dad and asked why they were asking for money.

He said, "They probably have no job or anywhere to live so they have to beg so they can at least eat."

To which I replied, "Why doesn't anybody help them?"

"A lot of people think they're just lazy and rely on people's goodwill so they don't have to work. But they obviously have their own struggles that stop them from becoming a part of society. That's why we should treat everyone with kindness, because we don't know what struggles they have or what ordeals they may have been through."

I fully understood this, but the difference with me was that almost everyone knew what I was struggling with, yet I was rarely treated with kindness.

I asked Dad, "Should we give them some money then?"

"If you want to, you can," he said, and gave me some coins to give. "I'm not sure D. B. Cooper needs your charity though. You'd think he still had something left from his heist."

He'd recently watched a documentary about this D. B. Cooper. Mum laughed but I had no idea what he was talking about.

I put my hand in my pocket and took out the pocket money I brought with me. I had a five-pound note and five one-pound coins.

In the distance, a man caught my attention. In a green khaki army cap, I wasn't sure if he was looking at me because he wore large dark glasses. I approached and gave him the five-pound note and the money Dad gave me.

It was when he thanked me I realised it was a woman. A gentle feminine voice, an unforgettable smile and gleaming white teeth behind not too plump lips. I heard a ping and there was a definite twinkle on her tooth, just like the toothpaste advert.

She gave my parents a nod of gratitude too.

I don't know why, but it felt so good to bring a little happiness to someone I thought so obviously in need.

We continued walking towards the shops through numerous parts of the shopping centre, and as we got through the large glass doors, there was something in the window a few shops ahead that caught my eye. I asked Dad if we could go into that shop and see what it was. He agreed but after he had bought shoes which were in the shop a bit further along.

As we were heading for the shop where his shoes were, we passed this item in the window of the gadget shop. I stopped dead in my tracks. It was mesmerising. A plastic ball with what looked like a steel ring inside flashing blue and red lights. I thought there must have been a motor inside it to keep it spinning as fast and as bright as it was.

Above it was a flashing sign:

TODAY ONLY

Brumalis

Lux version

£10 REDUCED FROM £40

Mum told Dad to carry on and get his shoes and meet us back there. I think she knew we would be in there for a while. I loved gadgets and the like and I told Dad to hurry back; he loved them too.

I looked again and noticed the ball was held by a stand, which was gently moving in a circular motion. We entered the shop and I asked the assistant what it was and how it worked.

He went to the window, took it out of the stand and returned to give us a demonstration. He continued the spinning of the wheel with the circular motion of his hands.

He said, "When I give it to you, move your hand in a slow circular movement, mainly from your wrist, and you will feel it exert a force. Slow and constant increases the speed."

As soon as I had a go, I was hooked. Intrigued by its inner workings, I wanted it.

Mum told me to wait until Dad got back, so I reluctantly browsed the rest of the shop until he arrived. Mum was really bored because gadgets did nothing at all for her.

When Dad arrived, I ran straight over to him, took his hand and dragged him to the counter.

I asked the man if Dad could try it. He bent down and took one from the counter underneath. Even the box was nice. It was a lovely shimmering blue colour with three gold dots on each surface. He proceeded to remove it from the box explaining that it wasn't really a toy but an aid to develop upper arm and wrist strength, speed and dexterity of the fingers.

"So, if you play golf, tennis or squash, it would be good for you as it'll strengthen your wrist and arm muscles," he said.

Being a keen golfer, Dad was always looking to improve his game. Even without trying it, he bought two. One each.

My parents still had a fair amount of shopping to do, so I had to wait until we got home before I could try it again.

On our return home, I helped them take their shopping into the house.

Well, not the shopping but the bag with the Brumalis in, and quickly took mine out of its box.

While Mum was preparing dinner, Dad and I were inspecting our new gadgets. Dad was reading the instructions while I was looking through the clear plastic outer casing trying to see the inner workings.

On finishing the instructions and explaining how it worked, we wound on the string and, after three, we pulled together. I didn't think I put my string on the wheel correctly because it tangled. Dad got his going straight away but stopped to put the string on properly for me. I pulled it again and it worked. The blue and red lights began flashing, not as rapidly as they did in the shop but the force coming from it was more intense than when I first tried it. So much so that I had to stop way earlier than Dad because my arm was aching so much.

After dinner, I tried to get Mum to do it but she couldn't get the rhythm of it like Dad and I, so she went back to the kitchen and finished tidying up.

Dad used his all the time. He obviously had his golf in mind. Even when he was watching TV, he would have his ball in his hand with his arm hanging over the side of his armchair slowly spinning it. It took me a while to master it but he spent a lot of time with me, trying to make me as good as he was.

Many evenings I played with this and though my attention was on trying to get it to go faster, my underlying thoughts were about how desperately in need of a friend I was.

It was the night of the full moon and, even though it was pouring with rain, I had occasional glimpses of it through the clouds.

Why don't people understand me? I thought as I stared at the moon. I really wanted to go somewhere I could be happy. Somewhere I wasn't judged.

The more I considered the cause of my sadness, the angrier I became.

Deep in thought, I subconsciously moved the ball in gradually decreasing circles and once I realised it was spinning faster than before, the blue light stopped and a constant red remained. I found this strange.

The shop assistant had demonstrated a ball spinning faster than mine, but I was sure the lights in his were always both colours.

As I continued to stare at the vibrant red colour, I went into a trance-like state. Then there was complete darkness.

What brought me out of it was the heat. The sun was blazing down on me.

Artemis

The first incident was over forty years ago, but I will always remember the tough life my family had. And not just my family, but the majority of the indigenous community all over our country.

As aboriginals, we were untrusted by nearby townspeople. We were victimised and generally disapproved of by society.

Whenever a crime was committed locally and no eyewitnesses came forward, the first call for the police would always be our community to question residents as to the whereabouts of the known criminals amongst us.

Our people were arrested consistently.

I remember Mum having an argument with a man in a shop on one of the rare occasions we went to the city.

I don't know if it was an unwritten rule for all stores, but every time we went shopping, without fail, we were always followed. Some made it blatantly obvious, while plain clothed security officers were a little more tactful.

I knew no different; I was a child.

I picked up a lolly as I held Mum's hand walking through the store. When she stopped to look at a coat, she let go of my hand. I stood at her side happily unwrapping the lolly. I was about to put it in my mouth when a man appeared in front of me.

In an attempt to stop me eating it, he grabbed my hand with great force.

That was when I had my first involuntary response.

With the surprise of this man seeming to appear from nowhere, I turned to him and shouted, "Wanker! Let me go."

That was my first Tourette's outburst.

I was as surprised as he was, but his reaction to my mother was very offensive.

"Typical. Just what I'd expect. You people are unbelievable, teaching your kids to steal at such a young age. Why is that? Hmm? You think you can get away with anything, don't you? You make me sick."

After Mum released my arm from his hand and calmed me down, she began to get so mad with this man I thought she was going to hit him. This was not a character trait I had seen from her before; she was normally a very calm woman.

During the commotion, a lady rushed over and, after seeing the guard's behaviour, a crowd began to form and soon after the head of security arrived.

On learning who this man was, the lady berated him telling him he should train his staff better in dealing with the public.

"This man is a disgrace," she said, pausing to look at the security guard's badge then continued, "I thought Derek was going to break the poor child's arm. If he treated a child of mine in that way, I would be suing him, you and the store!"

The situation was resolved pretty quickly after that. The security guard apologised as did the head of security and also asked if there was anything he could do. Mum point blank refused anything and said the best thing they could do was not tar everyone with the same brush. We weren't the stereotypes everyone made us out to be.

He apologised again and we left.

Situations like that at such a young age made me wonder about people. It left a lasting impression.

Mum rarely took me to the city after that.

Our traditional Noongar land stretched all the way from Geraldton, to Ravensthorpe in the south and inland to Southern Cross and we had family throughout.

Our culture is very different to the western world, and there are very few communities left that live the traditional way. So, I was lucky.

Our community is at Jurien Bay, and though the local town wasn't far from us, we rarely integrated.

Living a traditional life in a close-knit community, we all knew each other. Children were allowed to wander wherever they pleased, and being a coastal settlement, we were taught to swim at a very early age.

Mum enjoyed swimming too but the lack of comfort during pregnancy in the summertime forced her to walk to the billabong for a full body soak to cool off.

Stories of my birth at the billabong during the height of summer gave me my affinity with water, although it's possible it could have been the downpour that happened during the storm. But either way, being close to the ocean was good for me.

During the day, I would lie alone, daydreaming at the water's edge; the ebb and flow on the shoreline gently sending me deeper. Some days, the silence was broken only by the occasional small aircraft performing aerobatic manoeuvres, but instead of disruption, the sound blended with my thoughts.

Performing this ritual at night, with very little light pollution, gave me a connection to something. Something innate.

Absorbing the serenity of the ocean's whisper beneath the pin lit blackness, I was alone. But never alone.

Since my outburst at the store, the random shouting became a more regular thing. A lot of the time it happened due to my frustrations; they weren't always rude words and not really about what I was thinking, but nothing good ever followed them.

One time, Uncle came back without a turtle or any fish for the community, and as he was telling my mother about his fruitless day out in the boat, I shouted, "Bludger."

Words would just jump out of my mouth before I even realised what I was thinking.

I was told, in no uncertain terms, that this was not the way we treated our elders, or anyone for that matter. Our culture is about the respect for everything around us.

At that time, they didn't realise I had Tourette's.

In an attempt to control my outbursts, I would often spend time alone; sometimes on the beach, other times at the billabong.

Ours is fed by Jambarri River which flows all the way into the Indian Ocean, and when there are heavy rains, its course to the ocean becomes quite a torrent. Mum always warned me about it because the bunyip had been seen in most places along the river even close to the ocean which is unusual because they don't live in salt water.

"If you see any strange movement in the water moving, come home straight away. You don't want the bunyip getting you!" she would say.

The bunyip is a large mythical creature said to live in most inland billabongs, creeks and watering holes.

Many tourists are interested in our way of living and as a form of income to the community, the elders organise guided tours for visitors. Most have heard of Dreamtime and are curious to learn more, but the tours are more than that. The insight the elders give enables the tourists to see how we aboriginals live in harmony with the land and how it provides for us as well as the equivalent medicines that are found in nature, and how they are more effective than the chemicals they put into their bodies when illness strikes.

Every tourist group without fail would ask if there was a billabong they could visit. The closest was my solitary place, and quite often I would either hide or make my way back to Mum as soon as I heard them coming.

It was mainly adults, but occasionally there would be some children in the groups. This wasn't every day but we still had a lot of people visit our community.

Uncle would normally be the guide on these tours, but as he was travelling to Toodyay early the following day for an important meeting regarding ancestral land rights, he was making sure he had everything ready.

Doongarrah was to take the tour that day.

It was just after midday and I was lying in the sunshine. The silence was broken by children in the distance. I sat up and saw them coming towards me. I don't think they saw me as I quickly got up and went behind the nearby rocks. As I peered over, I could hear Doongarrah telling them of the billabong, how it wasn't there all year round because it was fed from the river, and unless there were heavy rains for a prolonged period, which had been common lately, it would be dry a lot of the time.

Once he'd finished, they began to make their way back. I peered over the rock then out of my mouth came a whistle and the words, "Go on, piss off!"

I immediately sat back behind the rock and waited a while longer wondering how I could try to control these outbursts. Once they were out of sight, I walked back over to where I was lying earlier.

I was almost there.

As I watched them leave, I kicked what I thought was a stone, but as I looked, it kept rolling and slowly gathered speed. I had to take a few quick steps but I managed to get hold of it.

I had no idea what it was, so I made my way back home to ask Mum, or whoever else was there.

As I walked into the village, I saw Uncle and showed him what I found.

It was obviously something new and modern but he had no idea what it was and said it was some sort of child's toy. I asked some others but still no one knew so I took it home.

It was a plastic ball with a wheel inside. With no idea what it was supposed to do, I tried to spin it by running the wheel over my palm while holding it by the outer casing. I ran it over my palm many times.

On my last attempt, it flickered. I thought I had better not let anyone see this or I would probably never see it again.

The following day, I went back to the billabong with the ball in a bag, so I could hide it. I knew it was a safe place for it because the only other people that went there were the tourists, and they were never there for that long.

The next time I went, it was the day after the hottest day we'd had in a while. Even at ten in the morning, it was about forty-two degrees. I was hoping it wasn't going to reach the fifty-six degrees of yesterday.

Still hot, I went for a swim prior to retrieving the ball.

I took it out of the bag and as I tried to spin it on my hand, the wheel wouldn't turn. With the heat of the previous day, and how I had jammed it under the large rock, the plastic casing had deformed a little and was pressing on the wheel. There was nothing around that I could use to prize it open, so I forcefully rolled it over my palm to see if I could get it to run freely again. As I was doing this, it slipped out of my hand and rolled into the water.

When I retrieved it, the coolness of the water had slightly shrunk the inner wheel and plastic casing and the wheel moved freely again, only this time, after a couple of spins, it continued on its own.

As I was turning it in my hand to see how this was happening, the original flicker of red and blue was now bright and constant, even in the intense light of the sun.

Startled by a red glow and a flash, I fell back.

As I got up, there was something different. What it was I didn't know, but I did notice the ball was no longer there.

Upset by this, I decided to go home, but in the searing heat, I decided on one last swim before I left.

After a quick dip, I took off my top to wring out the water and as I was stood there, I heard someone shouting, "Help!"

Phreya

I don't know if it was the heat, but the palm of my left hand began to burn intensely.

I stared at it. The symbol of the circle with the plus sign, arrow and arrow-plus sign reappeared. Curious again, I wasn't bothered by its reappearance, but more by the pain it caused.

I walked for so long I thought I would never see anyone. Thirsty because of the heat, I was about to give up when in the distance, I saw a girl stood by some large boulders. She was by the edge of the water with her top off.

I shouted at the top of my voice. "Help! Help me!"

The girl turned and made her way towards me as I ran to her.

Even though I started to cry when I approached her, she wasn't bothered about the state I was in at first, but more interested in what she said was in my hand.

She was asking questions about the ball and I was asking for water.

She took me to the place where she had been swimming and I jumped in.

It felt so good.

After dipping my head under the water, I lay on the shoreline with the water just covering my body. I lay there, wondering what had happened to me.

The girl enquired, "Where did you come from?"

"I don't know. I just ended up in the middle of nowhere and I've been walking for ages."

There was a long pause and then she said, "What's your name?"

"Phreya," I replied.

Still not really interested in the fact I wasn't from around here, she asked, "Where did you get that ball? I had one of those but it seems to have disappeared."

Though I couldn't see it, I knew exactly what she was talking about. At the same time, I could clearly see hers was in her hand but I told her about mine anyway, how it worked, what it did and how Dad and I were trying to get the most spins.

"How do you know how many times it spins?" she asked.

"It has a digital display on the top which records how many times it spins per minute."

I then told her of the one in her hand and, as she clapped her hands together, she said, "If there was anything in my hands, I wouldn't be able to this, would I?"

I asked her to clap her hands again and as she did, it looked as if the ball was made of light.

As she looked at me, I did the same.

We were both confused, yet amazed at the same time.

"What's your name?" I asked.

"Artemis," she replied. "But you can call me Arty."

"Arty, I'm really hot. Can we go somewhere to get a drink?"

"Do you want to come home with me? Are you hungry? Mum will feed you, and you can have a drink there."

I agreed and we made our way to her house.

While we were walking, she asked "Phreya. Is that a girl's name or a boy's?"

"Girl's," I replied quietly.

"Are you a girl or a boy?"

I repeated my previous answer.

"Why do you look like a boy then?"

To which I loudly blurted, "Because I don't want to be a girl."

To my complete surprise, she said, "Oh. Okay," and said nothing more of it.

I was so happy. No other child I knew had ever been this accepting of my choice. This made me forget almost completely that I was not from here. I really felt at home with Artemis.

Though I was hot and needed a drink, I also needed to pee. Her house must have been far away, because all I could see were tall fat trees, and I didn't think I could make it without peeing my pants.

She said we were in a special place because it was the furthest south these trees grew naturally and as no one else was around, I should go behind one of them.

Out of sight, I took down my trousers to squat down and pee. It felt different, and when I looked down, I had the shock of my life.

I called Artemis over. "Arty! Quick, come here and look at this!"

As she came around the other side of the tree, she said, "I thought you said you were a girl."

"I am! I mean, I was! I mean, I don't know."

Stood there with it in my hand, I was just staring at it as was she.

"What's happened to me?"

Though I was kind of happy, I was scared, because once again, I didn't know what was going on, but from then on, I could think of nothing else.

Artemis must have thought I was a liar and she didn't say a lot to me after seeing it.

I pulled up my trousers and we continued on our way.

We arrived at a village deserted, which surprised her, and the eerie silence broke ours.

We went into her house and she made us a cold drink.

"Do you want to come to my room?"

Which I did.

We tried to understand why we could only see and touch each other's balls and why they wouldn't leave our hands. She pulled mine so hard, she hurt my arm.

She then began to roll the inner wheel.

"What are you doing?" I asked.

"I'm trying to make the lights work."

"You don't do it like that. You need a piece of string to wind around the wheel and then you pull it, then move your hand in small circles to keep it going."

"Mine didn't need string. As soon as I got the lights to work, it kept going on its own. Try it," she said.

I ran my palm across the wheel of Artemis' ball faster and faster. The lights came on and then it continued on its own. As I watched, the lights grew brighter and the noise louder. The pitch reached the point where Artemis could hear it too. I decided to stop it because it was beginning to hurt my ears.

I asked her if she had any string or something like that so she could try to start mine.

The last thing I remember before I ended up there was playing with my ball.

If that's how I got there, maybe that's how I would get back.

We sat talking for such a long time, but still, no one came.

Artemis

We returned to my village with not a soul in sight. Something was wrong. The village was never empty.

I took Phreya to my house. Making our way to the kitchen whilst calling Mum, we checked every room, but there was no response. I made us a drink and went to my room, and after a long time talking, we tried to get each other's ball working.

She asked me to find a string to get hers started.

I hunted the house but couldn't find anything thin enough, so I went outside and found some old fishing twine. I went back in to get scissors and cut it to what I thought was long enough.

It took me a while but eventually I managed to wind it onto the wheel and with a sharp pull, the lights began to flash. Phreya started to move her hand in small circles and I could hear the wheel whirring as the lights became constant.

There was a flash, then she disappeared.

With no idea what just happened, I went to find Mum. I went into every house in the community but there was no one. It was like a ghost town.

We weren't that far from the local town but too far to walk so I spent that night alone.

I woke up the following day and still no one to be seen.

Getting worried, I decided to return to the billabong and I took my boomerang with me so I had something to play with.

I was there almost all day, playing and swimming, but I was getting hungry. I hadn't eaten since the previous afternoon and so I thought I had better go back to see if anyone was back at the village.

As I got up from near the water's edge, there was a ripple in the calm water. I moved a little closer to see what was doing it.

I slowly edged into the water and whatever it was got closer and closer to the surface and was moving with tremendous speed. The ripple on the water was moving faster and getting closer. Whatever it was breached the water not too far ahead of me.

I jumped back and stumbled. I fell onto my back, all the while watching this creature glide gracefully overhead.

I sat up and couldn't believe my eyes when I saw what lay ahead of me on the water's edge.

It wasn't what I expected a bunyip to be.

Phreya

After the flash, I didn't arrive in my room as quickly as I'd arrived at Arty's. This time, I was travelling along a winding tube at tremendous speed. I was glad my hair was short because the resistance from the speed was pulling at it so hard that if it was longer, it would have probably pulled it all out, though it did end up longer than when I began.

I managed to keep my eyes open, and ahead of me, I saw an apparition of my class teacher Mrs Osbourne.

Of all the teachers at school, she was the one who understood me the most. A very gentle lady who loved all her children. I felt she liked me most as she spent a lot of time talking and trying to help me understand why I was the way I was.

On noticing her, I forgot about travelling along this tube, and even though the resistance of my speed was still there, it was no longer uncomfortable. I felt calm and peaceful in her presence.

In her gentle voice, she said, "Hello Phreya."

I smiled nervously.

"There's nothing to be afraid of," she said as she motioned me closer, continuing with the loving smile she always wore.

She was my favourite teacher, but this was a random apparition. Everything about my recent experiences was very strange.

"You are a very special child, Phreya. As well as everything around you, I am a creation of your mind, and with the knowledge and power within you, you will experience that one desire that is so important to you.

"You have a great future ahead of you, and you will be an inspiration to many, because you will come to understand your situation in its entirety. Great changes will come. Not solely for you but the majority of your planet, and you are not alone in this.

"There are seven, one of which you have already met, and with your combined power and knowledge, for as long as you are a part of the seven, consciously or subconsciously, you will always be a force that can change the direction of nations.

"Everyone will benefit from your endeavours, but women more so. They have been held back for so long and the world has suffered because of this and when women of the world have been freed from the patriarchal chains that bind them, this will be the beginning of the new world.

"This is why the power from the light of winter is with you and the other six. It is at your command. Use it wisely."

It took me a long time to comprehend what I was told that night, but coupled with the revelation that I would experience my ultimate desire, I was excited for the future.

Crystal

Just moments before completely losing consciousness, every night, without fail, I hear a melody. I've never known any different. It's been a constant throughout my life, and only as my vocabulary grew did words accompany it. The words were always different but the feeling was consistent.

Until that night.

It was a voice like no other. Whenever I heard those soft gentle tones, I knew no harm could come to me. I felt safe. It calmed and soothed with its tranquillity, always bringing a feeling of peace.

It had the depth and mystery of the abyss, the smoothness and comfort of a silken cocoon, caressing every particle of my being with the clarity of the all-knowing.

How I love that feeling.

The difference that night was the mention of the word "Rendezvous". It evoked a different feeling. One of curiosity.

As a very young child, I believed the voice to be me. And why wouldn't I think that? They were my thoughts in my head. There was nothing or no one putting them there. It had to be me, because it was always there when I needed it. But after regaining consciousness, I realised it was something greater.

Lying unconscious on the playing field, I was surrounded by my classmates and teacher, wondering what had happened.

Mrs Webber lifted my head whilst saying my name, hoping I would come around. She checked my wrist for a pulse, which she found. With panic in her voice, she told Tracy and Gail to fetch the headmistress.

There was almost complete silence from my classmates, apart from Kevin and Jim, who once again were messing about and sniggering after Kevin suggested checking my pockets for sweets.

Not amused by this, Mrs Webber told the class to make their way back to the classroom, get their reading books out and wait for another teacher to come.

She saw Mrs Collins rushing over from the main building. She knelt down to take a look at me and asked what had happened.

"I'm not entirely sure. We were in the middle of our creativity lesson. I wandered between the students to make sure they were doing as instructed and everything was fine. I saw Crystal, and apart from being completely motionless, she seemed to be doing exactly as asked, so I continued through the group.

"When I was about halfway through, we heard this almighty thud from behind. It was so loud it got everyone's attention. We turned to see her, motionless on the grass."

After checking my breathing and turning me on my side, the headmistress told Mrs Webber to stay with me while she went to call an ambulance. All the while, I was observing every detail from above.

When I entered the kitchen that morning, Mum wiped the condensation from the window to see how Dad was getting on, but the outside temperature, the warmth of the central heating along with the cooking and the boiling kettle made the window quickly steam up again.

I could almost see the process. The window attracted the warmer moisture in the air like a magnet and, as it settled on the glass, it formed droplets, zigzagging their way to the bottom of the window, inevitably taking the path of least resistance. The droplets increased their speed as they attracted more of the same.

On finishing my breakfast, I went to the window and watched Dad through the hazy circular wipe marks.

I assumed the car was running with heaters on full blast in an attempt to warm it up inside and to help melt the frozen rain off the windscreen. At the same time, he was vigorously scraping the outside.

Intuitively, I knew.

He had that tell-tale furrow in his brow which always seemed to appear when he was in that kind of mood.

Freezing weather with no gloves, I could tell he was cursing under his breath, not just because of the weather but also for sleeping through his alarm, which he never usually did.

Mum, bless her, was always very patient with Dad, not that he was ever annoying. Well, not always, but when things were not "just so", it would sometimes fluster him and even the smallest annoyance could sometimes ruin his day.

If Mum wasn't around to put things back into perspective for him, he would have to take a nap, so he could re-evaluate the situation on awakening with a somewhat clearer mind.

That makes Dad sound a little needy, but he really wasn't. In fact, he was far from it, but that's what made them such a perfect match.

His occasional moments of minor meltdown always came at the time when Mum seemed to be at a low ebb and questioning her faith in her ability. Times like this helped her focus and hone her skills as a healer, not that he needed healing in any way, but whatever negative situation arose, the right words, feelings, emotions and actions would be expressed at the exact moment they were required by Dad and, without fail, she worked her magic every time.

Dad was meticulous in his approach to everything. Some would say he had OCD, but that wasn't him at all. It's just, in his world, if everything was where it was supposed to be, and he knew he could put his hands on it should he need to, then no panic would ensue, no time would be wasted and efficiency could continue. If I could describe him in one word that would be it: "efficient".

Where Mum would be deep in thought about the spiritual aspects of life, Dad would be deep in thought about what he saw as problems that needed solving. I don't think he really thought they were things that needed to be solved, he just loved pottering with random projects.

His latest project was clean energy. His vision was the creation of a power source that could self-generate.

At that time, I never knew where his ideas came from, nor did I know that this idea would eventually come to fruition, but the biggest surprise to me was that I was key or, more to the point, my ball was.

He didn't have the regular interests like my friends' fathers. He was far older and this may have been why. He never had an interest in football, being a member of any club or going to the pub.

Dad was a thinker. He did attend night classes on a few occasions, but that was to further his knowledge on electrical circuitry. It was never for the social aspect.

By normal standards, Mum and Dad left my conception late. They told me it was a conscious choice made for my benefit. They wanted to be able to afford themselves the opportunities to do what they wanted without the cloud of money worries hanging over them and when I arrived, they wouldn't have to work all hours to pay a mortgage and miss out on my formative years.

They wanted to look after me themselves, rather than leave me at day care or a child minder, which was the norm for my friends' parents.

Dad was twenty-five and Mum was twenty when they met. He was her postman. And she cared for Nan, my maternal grandmother.

It was a whirlwind of a romance.

Mum says it was love at first sight, but Dad says it like it is: Mum was hot! But whenever he talks of her, you can hear in his voice and see it in his eyes, he loves her deeply.

She is his world as he is hers. I believe it was love at first sight for him because he asked her to marry him within four months. They married on their seven-month anniversary.

As Mum was caring for Nan full-time, it made sense for them to move in with her, which was good for Nan too, because she loved Dad. When she remembered who he was.

Towards the end, the screaming episodes were becoming more frequent as the dementia grew worse. Mum told me when Dad came home from work, sometimes Nan would shout, "Ellen, Ellen! Quick, get Mortimer. There's a strange man just let himself in!"

And Mum would run down to the lounge only to find Dad trying to calm her down. I didn't know Dad's name was Mortimer until I was almost five; no one ever called him that, he was always Morty.

Seven years after they were married, Nan made her transition to the non-physical. After her passing, they struggled to stay on at the house. It was a Provincial Rental Housing property with only Nan's name on the rental agreement, and after a year of unsuccessfully trying to take on the tenancy, they decided to buy their own place. They managed to save enough of a deposit to buy a two-bed property with a small mortgage to service, and when I say small mortgage, I mean in terms of years not amount of money.

When eleven years were up of the twelve-year mortgage, that was the time I was conceived. Just after Dad's forty-fifth birthday.

Mum always sang to herself, but when she found out she was pregnant, the song she sang more than any other was "If I Can Help Somebody". But it wasn't just the singing. She was a spiritual woman with beliefs in many things. I think subconsciously she wanted me to feel the importance of the words she sang, the colours she surrounded me with and the remedies of old.

It was her way of ingraining compassion within her child, which without, I believe would have made my life adventures with the six almost meaningless. My knowledge of these things was to become essential in the navigation of my forthcoming dimensional travels.

Even before I could understand, she would surround me with a colourful environment. Whether it be toys, cushions or blankets, the colourful items were coordinated well.

She knew how to enhance the way I felt, especially when illness struck; her herbal remedy was like nectar.

That alone was worth being ill for.

—o—

Because Dad was late getting up, he took me to school. He called work to say he would be late, that way he would miss sitting in the traffic jam.

On the short journey, we talked about Christmas, what I wanted and what I might get, but there was only one thing I really wanted.

Dad dropped me off at the gates, watched me go in and then went on his way.

Once registration was done, Mrs Webber asked for three volunteers. Immediately I put my hand up as did Tracy and Gail. We were sent to the craft cupboard to get pegs and balls of string. We returned with our hands full, trying to put them all in the basket without dropping them.

It was the last day of term and maybe that's why a quarter of the class didn't turn up.

There were a number of things that had to be done throughout the school prior to closing down for the Christmas break, so volunteers were asked for.

Seven volunteered and that left only fourteen children, so instead of the usual last day of term movies, we had a creativity day, and it was quite different from the ones we usually had.

The weather was dry so we were going to have our lesson outside on the playing field.

"Right, now that you all have your coats and gloves on, get your books and pencils. We're going to the playing field." Mrs Webber picked up the basket of string and pegs and said, "Follow me, and the last person out, close the door."

It was a sunny, but cold winter's day. Mrs Webber took us all to a part of the field that was sheltered from the gentle breeze by a tall hedge. She laid out some picnic blankets she'd brought from home, so we could sit without getting our bottoms damp.

Once we were all sat and quietened down, she began.

"Today's creativity lesson is going to be one with a difference. We're not going to be making anything physical that we can touch. However, you will be able to take it home with you."

We all looked at her a bit odd because we couldn't figure out how we could make something that wasn't there yet still take it home with us.

"Can anybody guess how we can do this?"

Everyone was muttering amongst themselves, and someone shouted, "Magic."

Most of us laughed, as did Mrs Webber, but intuitively I knew, to take something with us that we couldn't see or touch had to come from within. So, I put up my hand and said, "Imagination, Miss?"

Most of the class looked at me just as oddly as we previously looked at her.

"Well done, Crystal," she said.

I was happy I was right. I had a very vivid imagination.

She continued "What we are going to do today is, each of you will choose a patch of grass and for about two minutes or so, you will look into it, and I don't mean stare. I mean really look, but before you do, in order for this to be as effective as possible, we have to have our minds as clear as possible. Try not to think of anything, not what you want for lunch, not what somebody said to upset you, not even what you're thinking Santa will bring you next week. Remember, the clearer your mind, the freer your imagination can be."

I heard some of the boys behind me whispering to each other.

"This is stupid, why doesn't she just let us play football or something? Or at least go back into the classroom. It's freezing out here!"

Although some of the girls weren't really interested in doing it, it was generally most of the boys.

"To help you have a clear mind, we'll do a breathing exercise and when I say go, you will begin to look and imagine."

After giving out the pegs and string, she said, "What I want you to do is push one peg in the ground, tie one end of the string around it, then press as many of the other pegs as you want into the ground and make a shape by winding the string around them, making sure you have a space in the middle. You can make any shape you want. Once you're finished, we shall begin."

Many weird and wonderful shapes were being made. For some of the girls, they took inspiration from Miss Collins' needlework and macramé lessons. With a needle and cotton, she taught us how to make curves with straight lines on a felt covered piece of card.

Mine, however unintentionally, turned out in the shape of a crown. It was by no means the best shape nor the most elaborate, but I liked it.

Mrs Webber walked around giving praise to all and once we were done, she sat in front of us and began.

"Okay, children, pay attention. The breathing exercise I mentioned will help clear your mind and give you a better experience, and it won't take too long."

Behind me, I heard Kevin say to Jim, "What's the point of this? I already know how to breathe!"

They burst out laughing.

Mrs Webber took it in her stride and calmed them once again.

"Okay, I'll tell you when to breathe in and breathe out, and when I think you're all ready, I will say, 'begin', then lean over your shape and stare as deeply as you can into it. I will give you three minutes to do this, then you will write one word in your exercise books to describe your experience. Are we all ready?"

Most of the girls said an enthusiastic yes and four of the boys gave a reluctant yes.

"Right, make sure you're sitting comfortably, close your eyes and try to clear your mind."

She began.

"Breathe in, breathe out, breathe in, breathe out. While you continue to do this, try to focus on something that will keep your mind from wandering. Breathe in, breathe out, breathe in, breathe out. Listen to the breeze, breathe in, breathe out. Hear the leaves on the trees quietly rustling, breathe in, breathe out, breathe in, breathe out. Listen to the birds singing, breathe in, breathe out, breathe in, breathe out."

It was very calming and peaceful, even the boys were quiet for a change.

Once she could see we were all ready, she told us to look into our shapes.

First of all, it was just the grass, then I noticed the dew glistening in the sunlight, also there was something that looked like beetle larvae. Then I noticed some movement. I thought it was odd at this time of year but I saw the tail end of a worm disappearing into what I guess was its burrowed hole. As the end of it disappeared, I slightly moved my head to see farther down the hole before it disappeared.

No sooner had I tilted my head, there was a sudden crack, like a discharge of electricity. Though my body stayed completely still, I felt like I jumped out of my skin. It felt as if my consciousness was being dragged from my body with such force and speed that I would never get back to it.

I was being dragged down the worm hole.

The blackness was so intense. It was like I was in the middle of space, but with no stars, planets or galaxies. The blackness was complete. There were no points of reference. I was suspended, motionless in the middle of the abyss.

In the distance, stars, planets and galaxies began to appear. I don't know what the speed of light is, but I'm sure I was going faster than that.

Then there was stillness.

It began as a hum, then a pulsing rhythmic vibration.

After listening a while, the hum and vibration evolved into words. That's when I heard it.

Eventually, I could make out my name. Slow, consistent and rhythmic.

"Crystal, Crystal, Crystal." It was the familiar voice I always thought was me. Only this time, I knew it wasn't. I wasn't in my body, so it couldn't have come from inside my head. And why would I call my own name anyway?

Initially, I was in utter oblivion. I felt extremely scared as I didn't know what was happening to me. Then a calmness came over me and I felt as if I was being guided towards something.

Once I understood the vibration, it started speaking to me.

"We are source energy. We are simultaneously everything, everywhere, eternally. The physical you is an extension of that which we are. In essence, you are us. We are one."

The voice continued. "For that reason, we are you, always with you, and always in appreciation of you. Relishing the changes brought with your every breath and every thought. Though your consciousness is a constant, it is eternally changing, and the changes are its experience and form, including everything in between and everything you believe to be outside of it.

"Your experiences will determine your form and your form will determine your experiences. In the physical, your consciousness cannot recall the experiences of previous incarnations. However, in the non-physical, the accumulation of all previous experiences will determine the next overall form, in anticipation of desired experiences. Prior to your incarnation, you knew what potential lay ahead in the direction you chose, and it is the desire within that will appear to put you in the right place at the right time.

"From the idea of you, to the conception of you, to the creation of you, it isn't just you that is responsible for this, for you are a tiny, yet integral component in the mystical collaboration of all desires.

"Your only aim is joy and to live a life where you can consistently achieve this will ensure it's a joyous one. And that which brings the most joy is what you do genuinely, whatever it may be. Not for reward but for the sheer enjoyment of doing it.

"There are those who believe that when the physical form is taken, it is for the learning of lessons, which are often repeated over and over, and once learnt, if ever, during incarnation, will enrich your soul, which works very well for most, but consider living life for the joy that it was meant to be.

"Either way, lessons will be learnt, the full range of emotions will be felt and you will be enriched from what you live, however you live it. But to do it purposefully will bring a deeper meaning to your life. It would be the choice we would make.

"For many generations, children have been, and still are, taught their parents' beliefs, which in turn become their own, and because your peers are your teachers, you accept what they say as the truth. That may be the case, but it is their truth and not yours, yet the majority of you don't begin to question your beliefs until you become independent and realise their beliefs don't fit with your perception of the world. This stirs something deep within, and the time is fast approaching for you, where this realisation will come to pass.

"The catalyst could be anything. It may be a smell, it may be a song, words in a book or an uninterrupted view of nature, but once everything is aligned, we will be waiting for the most important component of all. *You.*

"Simply put, it is a thought process and it will shape the rest of your life. It is all you. Your choices and timing. For most, it will happen, not just when it's least expected, but it will be a bolt from the blue, like a revelation that only you understand.

"You will feel as if your conscious perception is ripped from your reality and sucked into your mind by a force of limitless power. All around you will be a coalescence of universal entities swirling, collaborating, attracting, repelling, exploding, imploding. Everything and nothing all at once, and then you're back in your reality wondering what just happened.

"Only those who are ready will experience this. Those who want it will say you're lucky, those who don't understand will say you're not in your right mind. But whatever it is and whenever it happens, you will be ready and you will know it is a gift! Don't make this a quest and go looking for it. For those who consciously look will never find.

"Source energy responds to all things at all times. It gathers all cooperative components to fulfil all desires, from all forms of consciousness everywhere. Believers or non-believers, you all either have or will question our existence. Some call on us when in the depths of despair, some when in the throes of joy with gratitude but know this. We are always there. You just have to allow us.

"Though we have the power, we never force. We always flow along the path of least resistance. You just need to stop resisting. All life is a path of discovery, full of opposites and therefore balance; it's a journey to remember who you are.

"There are opportunities everywhere. They may appear scary, they may appear irrelevant but still opportunities. Recognise them, act on them, because they will keep presenting until you do.

"Time has come for the next incarnation of masters. However, this time, it is not just one. It is seven. And you are one. Do you believe you are ready? If you do, recognise the opportunity, grab it and hold on for the time of your life.

"It will be your lack of resistance, your desires and your allowing that will attract you to our message, and only those ready will become the seven. Dare to believe!"

—o—

When I realised once there is desire, travel in that realm was as instantaneous as the recollection of a memory. Just like the memory of a holiday. The moment you remember it, your mind is there, and no sooner had I thought about what happened leading up to being here, I was back in the school field; not in my body, but floating above and observing, and the most amazing things I saw were the colours around everybody's heads.

I wasn't sure at first, but after listening to their words, I realised it was their thoughts forming.

Initially, with all of them, it was just a mist, but as I continued to stare at each person, I began to see the individuality of each thought that made up the mist as they slowly started to separate. Though they were all the same thing, they were all very different.

I witnessed the separation of them as their colours started to break through and they looked like they were wearing crowns, very beautiful in form but occasionally the colour of some went quite dark momentarily, with only a few glistening specks.

As a very strong-willed person, Tracy's crown had an underlying shade of red, and Gail, with her vitality, excitement and sociable traits, her base colour was orange.

Kevin was very intelligent with a positive attitude and an abundance of energy, the yellow of his was so intense I could almost feel it, and with the blue of Jim's, I assumed this colour meant loving, caring, and a speaker of truth, because that's exactly how I knew him to be.

Though I knew nothing of colour psychology at that time, I interpreted the colours I saw as good or not good.

Mum gave me a very basic explanation of the colours she would surround me with, and this became the basis of my judgments. How they made me feel. This became a very useful guide for me.

The colour of their thoughts was a direct indication of how I knew them to be, and also, I could tell their mood from what I saw.

I was amazed at the range and speed at which thought moved. Positive thought was very colourful and moved circularly at a slow constant speed, whereas the spectrum of negative thought was from the lightest grey to the blackest black, but moved at immense speed.

Most of my classmates looked as if they were wearing dull crowns, and the way the negative thoughts were shooting in and out looked like thorns.

The tops of their heads were the most beautiful colours I had ever seen, but the speed at which the negative light grey thoughts were shooting in and out of their heads really dulled the vibrancy of their base colour. Yet their crowns were still a thing of immense beauty.

At that moment, I felt my consciousness throw itself towards my body. I had been so focused on all I was witnessing, the impact of it plunging back into my body threw me far behind where I was kneeling.

I hit the ground with a loud thud and due to the pain from my heavy landing, I lost consciousness once again.

My short life up until that morning was one which I would describe as complete happiness. At no point do I recall any upset at home. Come to think of it, I don't recall encountering any elsewhere either, and wanting a balanced and non-judgmental life for me, Mum taught me her interpretation of holism. She loved God, but didn't want me getting lost in the dogma of religion. She always made it fun.

At the time, I believed we were playing together, but that was her way of teaching me without my knowledge of it. The initial game was one of our favourites.

Being subjected to this way of thinking from birth, it was inevitable my knowledge of anything spiritual would be far greater than that of my school friends.

I regularly heard things like characteristics of living, esoteric traditions, chakras, supernatural and the like.

For the initial game, we would think of relevant words beginning with the first letter of our names. Every word or phrase I said was explained to me.

Mum always made me feel like a high achiever because she would say, "Hmm, I can't think of many things beginning with E."

Her games with me embedded an invaluable knowledge, subsequently making me aware of what I was a part of.

Was this her way of preparing me for my life ahead?

Some of the children at school thought Mum was a bit hippy and would occasionally mock me by doing hippy dances, but that was mainly the boys.

It didn't bother me because I understood.

To me, my parents were, and still are, the epitome of parenting. They were loving, nurturing, caring and understanding. All the things a child needs.

But no matter how loving my home environment was, I doubt there was anything anyone could have done to prepare me for the encounter I woke up to early the following morning.

It was past midnight. I sat bolt upright whilst inhaling the largest breath. My heart was pounding so hard my whole body was throbbing, raising my temperature so high I thought I would explode. My stomach violently twisted in knots to the point I could hardly contain the impending vomit.

With such a violent awakening, I didn't know if I was dreaming or not.

Eyes open wide like saucers, I took in as much information as I could, about my surroundings. I was attempting to figure out where I was, and whether or not I was dreaming.

I thought I woke up, but wasn't sure.

Is this real? I thought. *I hope so!*

With my attention so fixated, thoughts of reality soon left. This bedroom was so warm, peaceful and cosy. Constellations in luminous paint on the ceiling, one battery-operated candle gently flickered on the sill, surrounded by healing stones of crystals and quartz.

From the headboard of my bed, following on each of the six walls, was a wavy musical staff with notes painted on them, as if the music was dreamily emanating from my head and circling the room.

The solitary dreamcatcher shimmered above the flickering light of the candle, and as I sat up, the facing wall below the strange eighteen-hour clock was an unusually large luminous mandala with the figure eight at its centre.

I had the strangest ability to focus intently on two separate and completely different things. While becoming mesmerised by the mandala, I was carrying out calculations instigated by the clock.

Time as I knew it was subjective, and how I experienced it was dependent on my mental state. Shock, disbelief and incomprehension slowed my perception of time, whereas surprise, ecstasy and euphoria passed it far quicker.

I figured this was due to understanding.

I needed more time to understand what I didn't understand, and less time to understand that which I loved, because I knew love was my connection. It was innate.

This dream had both. Simultaneously. Less and more combined.

If only this perception could be controlled.

As I absorbed my surroundings, I grew calmer. My mind began to slowly remember and comprehend the difference between dreams and reality.

Most times on awakening from any kind of dream, it fades quickly, but the vividness of this one I remembered everything about.

That dark early morning was the turning point in my life.

The feeling I had in the pit of my stomach on awakening that morning was one of panic, fright and complete fear. I had no idea why I felt that way.

What I now knew was a dream was serene, even my experience at school was a pleasant one, but then I remembered the force at which my consciousness returned and the pain as I hit the ground. The good and bad of both experiences sent my mind on an emotional rollercoaster.

I wasn't feeling too good yesterday after my bodiless experience amongst the stars. Even though my body wasn't with me, my mind must have brought something back because within hours, there was a quick onset of a cold.

Mum commented on how ill I looked when she picked me up, and I gradually felt worse as the day went on. That night, without having dinner, and an hour earlier than normal, I headed for bed at seven o'clock.

My eyes felt like they were drooping over my cheeks and my nose was so blocked I could only breathe through my mouth. I had trouble breathing all that night, and I was sure there would be a headache to follow.

After I had drunk most of Mum's homemade shiver-inducing cold remedy, I grabbed my knitted mermaid tail blanket and ball, and went off to bed.

Though I wasn't feeling great, I wasn't so tired that I could go to sleep immediately, so with ball in hand, I thought I would attempt to beat my record of revolutions. My current record was 1111 revolutions per minute.

Sat on the side of my bed, I put the string's aglet into the hole located at the centre of the inner wheel on the underside of the ball, and wound it on carefully.

With one quick pull, the revolutions began and, with dim lights, the gentle force was instant.

Three times I tried to beat my score, but the amount of time I spent on each attempt made my arm ache so much, I decided to leave it for another day.

With most of my energy now drained, I managed to pull on my mermaid tail and climb into bed. I snuggled up under my little mermaid duvet and fell asleep.

I slept lightly that night for quite a few hours, until there was a thud on the floor. It wasn't very loud, but being restless, it woke me.

I continued to lie there trying to sleep. Eyes still closed, I turned to face the window. Beginning to drift, for the second time that evening, the melody came. The words were different again.

"Look beyond the veil, open your eyes and dive right in."

Almost asleep, it took a while for the words to register. This repeated until I eventually opened my eyes. A little at first as the darkness slowly faded. The slit between the curtains caused a faint veil of light to partition my room.

From my side of the veil, I noticed the ball on the other. It landed in the path of the moonbeam as it shone through the gap in the curtains.

The light caught the slightly protruding edge of the wheel that lay at its centre.

Still in my mermaid tail, not wanting to wake Mum and Dad, I got out of bed, slowly and quietly. Manoeuvring myself close to the window, I picked it up.

The string wasn't with it.

There wasn't a lot of light in the room and I couldn't see it and I tried to remember where I dropped it when I last pulled it.

On all fours, quiet and slow, I lightly moved my hands across the carpet and beneath the edge of my bed trying to find the string. I felt around, gently patting my hand on the floor, until I felt the end of it.

Once retrieved, I moved back into the moonlight so I could find the hole and get the string wound on. Once again, one quick pull and the normally dim lights appeared to be a lot brighter in the darkness, and with the gentle whirr of the wheel, I started the circular motion. This time without the earlier strain and exertion, I eventually reached an easy rhythm to keep the wheel going for as long as I wanted.

I don't know how long I was doing this, but Mum's song began to play. I was staring at the mandala and quietly singing to myself, appreciating the intricacies of the geometric shapes that made it up, and watching how the figure eight became an infinity symbol twice on every rotation.

I must have gone into a trance or some kind of meditative state, because I could see its circles moving; more precisely, it was the centre circle. It separated into three parts.

There were three breaks in it: one at the top, and the other two were at bottom left and right. As they slowly moved apart, they formed three increasing arcs individually circling themselves. During their motion, one end stayed in place and the other end swung to the centre where they joined. It looked like a curvy three-pointed star inside a circle.

Once the centres were joined, it began to spin. Slowly at first, but as it grew faster, the next outer set of circles began to spin. It was as if each outer set of circles would start to spin once the previous set had reached their zenith.

I now know this coincided with the speed at which my ball was spinning: 1,618 revolutions per minute. The space between each of the three points flashed one, six and one, together with the eight at its centre was the number on the ball's digital display.

This continued until the whole geometry of it was spinning. Then in the blink of an eye, there was darkness.

What happened at school yesterday, happened again.

Only this time, when I emerged from the statically charged tunnel, I was swimming under water. It felt so natural, there was no struggle at all.

Without using my arms, a gentle kick of my legs would propel me quite a distance for the amount of effort put in. It was almost effortless.

There was very little resistance as I glided past coral reefs and shoals of fish, enjoying the beautiful sights around me. I saw such a variety under the ocean that day. There were turtles, starfish, blue ringed octopuses and a whale shark. I loved every moment of that experience.

I turned and had the most wonderful surprise. It almost brought me to tears.

I was a mermaid.

My scales were the most beautiful iridescent dark blue, glistening in the beams of sunlight as they reflected. They gradually got lighter as they reached my tail, which was very muscular, then trailed off into a silk-looking membrane billowing in the current of the water as I swam.

I swam in circles for a while just to admire the beauty, then continued exploring.

In awe of all beneath the waves, something caught my eye. Too far to distinguish, I swam closer. I didn't seem to have my normal mindset, so never considered the possibility of sharks.

Getting ever closer, I could make out their form.

A pod of dolphins playing, powering through the water, breaching the surface, before their graceful re-entry.

As I considered joining them, I sensed something gaining on me. I looked back only to see another two dolphins heading directly at me. I stopped swimming.

As they reached me, they slowed and began to swim in spirals around my length, from my tail to my head. It went on for a while, but when they stopped, they both stared directly into my eyes.

I smiled. Though they always look like they're smiling, I felt they were too as they nodded before swimming off in the direction of the pod. I felt I should follow.

My body was very efficient as it glided through the water with what was a very powerful tail.

We played together for some time, then they swiftly departed. Unsure why, I turned to explore more.

As I straightened up, I was face-to-face with a great white shark. The surprise of that encounter made me inhale sharply even though I was underwater. The whole time, I never considered how I was getting my oxygen, and being startled in this way, I realised it wasn't by breathing. The stabbing pain was so intense throughout my lungs, I thought I would pass out.

Luckily for me, the shark was just being inquisitive, otherwise I would have been its meal for the day, but not knowing that, I swam frantically towards the light at the surface.

It felt like an eternity.

My lungs were ready to explode when I breached the surface. I was travelling at such a speed that I glided through the air like a siren and landed just on the shoreline.

The attempt to empty my lungs caused violent painful coughing. My throat felt different, like it was full of tiny hairs as I coughed up the water and almost vomited in the process.

I lifted my head and directly in front of me was a girl. She looked as surprised to see me as I felt on seeing the shark.

The girl, who looked the same age as me, came over and helped me to sit up. She began patting my back thinking it would help bring up the swallowed water, but it felt more like she was trying to smash my spine with a stone right between my shoulder blades.

As I screamed in pain, she stopped and sat in front of me.

"You're far more beautiful than they told me the bunyip was," she said.

"What? What's a bunyip?" I asked.

She moved beside me, and as she ran her fingers through my hair and over my scales, she said, "It's a strange beast that lives in watering holes. I've never seen one before but you are a beautiful one."

"I'm not one of them. I'm a girl! And where am I?"

"Jurien Bay," she said casually.

"Where's that?"

"What? Australia, of course."

In utter shock, I said to her, "How did I get here?"

It was then she noticed the ball in my hand.

"I don't think you're from here."

"There was a boy here yesterday who had one of those magic balls."

She proceeded to tell me all that happened with this boy, and how he eventually disappeared.

It was then I realised what the pain was when she was patting my back.

Once she told me this, everything fell into place. I remembered the ball, the mandala and the music. I felt I knew everything.

"I don't think you're from here either," I said. "Have you seen anyone else with one of these balls?"

"No, just you, me and Phreya. What's your name?"

"Crystal, but don't call me Chris, I never answer to that. My last name begins with C so some people call me CC or Sissy too. What's your name?"

"I'm Artemis, but you can call me Arty."

"Is this where you live?" I asked.

"About ten minutes' walk that way." She pointed beyond the trees in the distance.

"Is there anything different about this place?" I asked, trying to figure out if we were in the real world or not, because there was no way I could get to Australia so quickly and not know how.

"I was playing with my ball yesterday when Phreya arrived. She said she was a girl, but I saw it. She was definitely a boy. I took her back to the village, but it was deserted and I haven't seen anyone since."

I thought these balls must be some kind of time machine. Either that or something that made us experience vivid and very real dreams.

Though the sun was going down, it was still very hot.

Arty said she was going for a swim again and asked if I wanted to join her. I thought I should as my scales were beginning to get very dry.

Awkwardly shimmying my bottom along the sand as I made my way back to the water's edge, I almost heard my scales sing with a sigh of relief as I sat there up to my shoulders.

Arty was swimming. I was dipping my head in and out of the water to see if I could breathe under water. I thought I must be able to, because I was fine until I saw the shark.

I thought back to when I was looking around under the ocean and remember taking water in and out and it must have been the hair-like tufts in my throat helping me to breathe. I dipped my head in the water and nervously took in some water.

Again, I coughed, but not as violently as before.

Arty swam over to me to see if I was okay, and after a few more attempts, I managed it without coughing. Then I went for a swim.

I came back to Arty, took her hand and swam her through the water.

She was good at holding her breath. We went under the water and looked at everything. We were joined by a pod of dolphins which again seemed to appear from nowhere. They were very inquisitive and playful, jumping out of the water and racing back and forth along the shoreline.

I was now having so much fun I decided to copy the dolphins and breach the surface. The feeling I had flying through the water then the air was electric, but the re-entry was painful so I didn't do that again.

The sun was beginning to set and the light was fading very quickly. We were growing tired after all the swimming, so we got out.

Once the sun had set, it got dark very quickly, not like at home. It was almost pitch black by this time and too dark for Arty to walk home, so we decided to stay put until sunrise.

Sat with my tail in the water, which thankfully was warm, and with Arty by my side under the light of the moon, we sat talking for a long time, mainly about the balls.

I told her my thoughts about them and we were coming up with a lot of ideas of what we could do if we were right about their capabilities.

Arty was very interested in her history and wanted to learn as much as she could about it. She said, "We could go back in time and meet our ancestors and find out more about the Dreamtime."

Having never heard of this, I asked her what did she want to know about dreaming.

She seemed a little affronted by this and told me the Dreaming or Dreamtime was about creation according to Aboriginal culture.

I considered this for a while. Being my first adventure with my Brumalis ball, I wasn't sure it was a time travelling device so I asked her if she thought she had travelled through time.

She thought about this for a few moments. "I can't really say for sure, and I don't know how I would know. But wouldn't it be good if we could?"

I agreed. I wouldn't have changed the experience I had in school, but I would prepare myself for my consciousness coming back into my body so I didn't experience the pain of the landing.

I tried to keep our conversation serious but Arty was on a roll.

"Or what about going to different planets and meeting aliens? Or travelling the whole universe?" Then after a short pause, in an intriguing and mischievous tone, she said, "What about finding God and asking her a few questions?"

I laughed so much. She had an imagination as vivid as mine, but that comment brought to mind something my mother had told me. I didn't want to say it, but I couldn't not tell her.

"Why do you say 'her'?"

"Mother Earth," she replied.

"My mother told me God is not what people have been taught it is. She said there is no gender or judgment; there is only love and being taught anything of what God may be stops you from learning what God is for you."

When Mum told me this, she also said, "To some people, God is non-existent." She didn't elaborate and, at the time, I didn't ask why or what that meant.

We stopped and thought about that for a while.

But then Arty continued. She had me rolling with laughter through most of our conversation. So much so I gave very little input, but eventually, she got serious and told me of how aboriginal people have been treated over the years. Though she hadn't endured much of it herself as she was so young, some of the stories she'd overheard from her elders and others in her community made her sad. Her emotions were strong.

I listened intently as she told me of a time she went to the city with her mother. Her mood went from sadness to anger and she seemed to enter an almost trance-like state. I noticed her ball began to flicker.

She continued. "I don't know why they don't like us. We're no different to any other race of people. We have good and bad, the same as them. It must be because of our skin colour."

I really didn't know what to say to her so I put my arm around her and gave her a hug.

She then said, "If that security guard could experience life as an aboriginal, I'm sure he wouldn't continue to treat us the way he does."

Then out of the blue she whistled, made a clicking noise with her mouth and said, "I. M. Bude ain't gonna like that."

"Ain't gonna like what?" I asked.

Her reply of "What?" made me wonder if she knew what she had just said.

We said no more and lay down.

Lying on our backs looking up at the stars, I suddenly remembered the voice and my journey down the worm hole.

I said to Arty, "This is a good thing. We're meant to have fun with this."
She replied, "I am ready."

I repeated her words, and no sooner had the words left my mouth, two shooting stars blazed across the night sky. We took that as a sign, and of all the things we dreamt up together that night, they were nothing compared to our scary first adventure with all seven.

The sun rose the following morning and there was still no sign of any adults. I said to Arty we should try to get out of here or back to our own realities, or we would die with no food and no adults around, but we needed a string or thin lace to start our Brumalis balls.

She said she didn't need a string and told me how her ball worked.

I thought that was lucky as we didn't have one anyway, so I listened to her instructions and started hers.

I thought it would be difficult to get mine to start with hers, but as we were slowly moving them closer, assuming they were the same size, shooting from them and disappearing straight away were not sparks but what looked like small replicas of the shooting stars we saw the night before.

Once it had stopped emitting these little stars, I assumed both wheels were turning at the same speed, so I took my hand away and started doing small circles.

I felt the force immediately, and as I looked up to tell Arty, she was gone.

In a slight panic, I concentrated on getting the wheel to spin faster and faster, because if this didn't work, I would be stuck here with no way of starting it again, and no way of getting home.

I felt a lot colder. I was home again.

Derek

After the warning received from the head of security, Derek was enraged even more. He didn't believe he'd acted in a way that was adverse to the store's policy and as far as he was concerned, he was doing his job effectively.

Still angry when he got home, he found it hard to settle. His wife tried to calm him by telling him he was right in his actions after he'd told her what had happened. This subdued him a little but it was on his mind for the rest of the evening.

The twelve-hour shift exhausted him, so he took a shower, had his dinner and went to bed.

With the following day being his day off, no alarm was set. He needed a good long sleep to refresh himself and hopefully forget about the day's incident.

His wife followed him half an hour later.

He was restless in his slumber and it took her a while to get to sleep, disturbed with swift arm movements and mumbled racist slurs.

She reached over for her earplugs. *This was going to be a long night*, she thought.

After an hour or so, he was woken by frantic screaming.

He opened his eyes to see his wife stood by the window brandishing a bedside lamp.

"What the hell's wrong with you?" he yelled.

He sounded different and while clearing his throat, terrified, she said, "Who the hell are you? What are you doing in my bed? Where's Derek?"

With exactly the same attitude and looking almost identical apart from a slightly larger nose, she didn't recognise him as her husband, she only saw his colour.

"For God's sake, Karen, shut up and get back into bed. You're having a nightmare again!"

"Get out or I'll call the police." She looked around the bedroom in desperate panic to find something else to use as a weapon.

"What's wrong with you?" he asked, "I'm Derek."

"My husband is not aboriginal!"

"Are you deliberately trying to wind me up because of what happened today?"

Frozen to the spot and unable to leave the room, she threw the lamp at him and picked up her nearby jewellery box.

He pulled the sheet up as her perfect aim directed the lamp straight to his head. Shielded by his arm, the globe broke falling onto the bed.

He rose from the bed and she cowered in the corner.

Upset by this, he went to the bathroom. Turning on the light, the mirror confronted him.

"What the he—Karen! Karen! What's happened to me?"

Not acknowledging his despair, she screamed again shouting, "Get out! Get out!" then she ran out herself, taking her mobile phone with her.

In complete shock, he finally left the bathroom and went to the lounge, only to hear her on the phone to the police.

Staring him straight in the eye and in a nervous voice, she was finishing her call.

"Yes, an aboriginal man... No, I don't know him. I've never seen him before... Thank you."

Ending the call, she said, "You'd better get out of here. They're on their way."

Knowing she'd called the police, he considered staying put and talking to them, but he was well aware of how aboriginal people were treated, so he decided to leave and figure out what to do later. He dressed quickly, grabbed his wallet and rushed through the door.

With nowhere to go, he wandered for a while and ended up sleeping the rest of the night in a bus shelter.

It wasn't the heat of the early morning sun that woke him. It was the prod of a walking stick.

Many people were waiting for the bus but none dared enter the shelter to shade from the sun while he was there.

An elderly man approached, walked straight into the shelter and, in no uncertain terms, told this presumably drunk, indigenous man to get out.

He wouldn't normally stand for this treatment from anyone, especially a stranger, but he remembered why he was there.

He got up and left without a word.

The fifty dollars in his wallet wouldn't last long and with his background and surveillance knowledge, he was reluctant to use his bank card.

Not in possession of ID and nothing to prove his real identity as well as the consequences of being caught as a home intruder and thief, he would be looking at a custodial sentence if apprehended. He thought about this possibility and knowing very little of aboriginal culture, he believed life in prison would be too tough for him and he didn't want to mix with them, but realised he would have very little choice.

His close friends had a similar mindset and treated aboriginals the same, so he couldn't call on them.

He was now alone in the world.

Over a few days, he only bought what was absolutely necessary, but such a dire situation drove him to spend the last of his cash at the Bottle-O.

Completely inebriated at another bus stop, he began abusing passers-by, blaming everyone but himself for his situation.

Drunk and alone, he fell asleep as darkness descended.

Early evening came and a young aboriginal couple noticed him as they passed. Unable to wake him and not wanting to leave him, they went to get their car.

Arriving back at their community settlement, the struggle to get him out was easier than getting him into the car as others came to help. Inala went in to make up a bed for him while Doongarrah helped to get him into the house.

In and out of consciousness, he spat a string of slurs towards his rescuers, but they continued to make him comfortable.

He woke before sunrise with no idea of his location and surroundings.

He wandered and found the kitchen. Unable to remember his last meal, he searched the refrigerator and cupboards. With no consideration for any that may have been in the house, his racket woke Doongarrah.

Knowing the source of the noise, he entered the kitchen.

"Good morning. How are you feeling?"

Taken aback by the calm welcoming exterior of the stranger, Derek became flustered.

"How did I get here? And who are you?"

Doongarrah explained the situation as he began to make a coffee.

"Would you like one?" he asked.

Derek accepted as Inala entered the kitchen. "Oh, you're up. How are you feeling this morning?"

"I feel okay."

Intimidated because of his surroundings and a slight discomfort because of his hosts, he remained courteous.

"Why am I here?"

They told him of the previous night.

Grateful for their compassion, he wondered what his future would hold.

Sat around the kitchen table, they began to talk.

"So, what mob do you belong to?"

He knew nothing of any of the aboriginal communities in any part of Australia, so his answer was, "I don't remember."

"What's your family name?"

With no knowledge of anything about aborigines, he thought his best course would be amnesia.

Their questions continued and his answers remained the same.

Doongarrah and Inala shared ancestral knowledge of the forty thousand years of being custodians of their land and, not wanting this man to leave them with no knowledge of it, they shared it at every opportunity. They spent months teaching him everything from the dreaming to aboriginal mythology to surviving the outback and the modern world.

He remained with them for over two months.

The knowledge shared with him left him in awe and wanting more.

His whole perception of the First Nation was turned on its head and, as a result, he knew he was a changed man.

That night, he went to bed with the intention of changing Australian society's perception of this beautiful nation.

The following morning, his alarm went off. Blending with his dream, it didn't wake him.

Then, with a gentle shake, he woke to the sound of, "Derek. Your alarm. Switch it off. It's time to get up. You have work today."

He woke with a start at the sound of Karen's voice.

Artemis

I had the ball in my hand and everything was back to normal again, except the time of day. I left Crystal just after sunrise but now the sun was far higher in the sky. It was more like after ten in the morning, so I made my way back home.

On arrival at the village, I saw Mum putting out some washing.

"Why are you back so soon? You've only been gone half an hour."

I was surprised by this as Uncle was also still there.

I asked Mum, "Did Uncle go to Toodyay yesterday?"

"No, that's early tomorrow morning," she replied. "What's wrong with you today?"

Then it hit me.

I realised there was little time difference, if any at all, between embarking on a journey and returning.

With that in mind, and knowing the ball was always with me, I decided I would try it again later alone in my room, but making sure I could always feel the force from the ball, so I could speed it up when I felt I needed to get back.

I started the ball and as the speed was increasing, most prominent in my mind was why were these things happening, why me and how did this all work.

My next journey wasn't as instantaneous as the first.

Before the darkness, I found myself travelling through an electrified tube and though there didn't seem to be any wind, the resistance around my head was so intense I thought it was going to pull my hair out.

There was darkness all around me. I might as well have had my eyes closed, but staring intensely into the abyss, I saw what looked like pin lights coming towards me. Slowly at first, then with immense speed.

I thought they were going to smash straight into me, but every single one passed me by, and as I turned to watch them, they disappeared into the distance.

I turned back to see planet Earth in all its glory with Australia dead ahead.

Still travelling at speed, I was getting scared. I could see Uluru directly below me.

With no way of slowing myself, death was inevitable. I thought it was going to be my last trip.

Fortunately, gravity didn't affect me until I was safely stood on solid ground.

Before landing on Uluru, I noticed there was something else on it. From a distance, plummeting with squinted eyes, it looked like a red kangaroo at first, but as I got closer, I could clearly see it was an elder. He had many patterns painted in white all over his body.

It wasn't until I was older, I found out this was Gambu Ganuurru, warrior and wise leader of the Gunnedah tribe.

I don't know how, but he made me feel so comfortable I felt I was equal to him in mind, body and spirit. Maybe that's why I understood most of what he shared.

After the traditional Welcome to Country, we sat together.

His voice was deep and with his velvet tone, he began.

"Artemis, it has been long, and we are happy to be meeting with you at this time. We will meet many times. We will have many forms and we will teach you many things. It is by your desire we are here today and we will help you understand."

I was unsure why he kept saying "we", but that understanding came eventually.

"This is a great beginning. The world has been waiting for you as it is on a path that is not promoting its wellbeing and as we do not interfere with the free will of anyone or anything, we have been waiting for the arrival of people who are willing to do what is necessary to show an alternative way of thinking. Not by force, but by example.

"The mind is the key. It is not where anything begins or ends. It is a place of fertility where thoughts can emerge, and if you tend to them regularly, your desires will grow, thrive and come to fruition. If you don't weed out the negative thoughts, they will take root, grow strong and choke your desire. You see, thoughts never die. They transform as they attract similar thoughts in order to become.

"Sometimes in this dimension, sometimes not, but always somewhere within the fabric of space and time. Within your mind, you are creating the conditions for a life without limits and, until now, there have only been a few that have succeeded. You call them masters. And now, time has come once again for change. This will be your first lesson and we will begin at this time with universal law. MEDITATE.

"First and foremost is the law of attraction. Meaning that which is like unto itself is drawn. From galaxies to single cell amoebas, this is how things become. It's how you became, and also how we are. Nothing is outside of this law, even what you may think is insignificant, attracts and is attracted to.

"Second is free will. Universally, beings make choices which they believe are best for them, so interfering with free will is not a choice we would make. You can attempt persuasion to change the mind of someone, but like yours, choice has to be from free will. No one likes to be forced to do what they don't want to do. Also, any force applied to anyone or anything, immediately creates resistance and distances you from us.

"Lastly, when you have inspired knowledge or a revelation, and all seven of you will have many, *know* that it is for you and you alone. If it was for anyone else, they would have the revelation too, and if you attempt to force any beliefs new or old onto anyone, it will be detrimental to you only, and will benefit them in no way at all. Never forget these three laws. CLARITY.

"As for the balls, there are many out there, but yours, Phreya's, Crystal's and four others are different, and that difference is one of the reasons we are here now. Within the Lux Brumalis, there is a tektite quasar at their core. A glass-like material that was caused to splinter from one of the tri star suns of the Empyrean Omnipote Plane located in a black hole within the Ubique galaxy.

"It is special because, firstly, it is unknown by man for anything to leave a black hole and, secondly, because of the infinite energy, power and knowledge within it. If humanity knew of this, it would be of far greater value than any precious stone or metal currently known. Not because of its hardness or iridescent beauty, but because of what it contains. That is why you always have to keep them safe.

"When you left the abyss, you split into seven equal parts. On leaving the black hole, the quasar also split into seven, but one part was double the size of the others, and that quasar is within your ball, so it is only you that can command all others to join you wherever you may be."

Throughout his sharing of knowledge, I was mesmerised by him and his presence, but once I had digested that last piece of information, my imagination went wild, imagining how to get the others to me, where it was we would meet, what the other four looked like, if Crystal would turn up as a mermaid, and if Phreya really was a boy.

I was brought out of my daydreaming by him gently but firmly saying, "clarity" again whilst staring to the heavens.

I then realised. The outbursts of random words were just like my Tourette's. But they had meaning.

He continued. "When you call for them, it is very important you meditate first. If you are not clear of mind, they will get to you, but they may travel through one of the many realities ever present in your mind.

"So, anything in your past that you have not come to terms with and still upsets you when you think of it, some or all of the other six may experience that too, and if it wasn't pleasant for you, it is unlikely to be for them."

I was worried about anyone enduring some of the things I had been through, but I put that out of my mind as he continued.

"When the seven join, the quasars will too, and at the moment of amalgamation, the information we have shared with you, and what you have learnt through experience individually, will be available to you all. So, all seven will always be prepared for whatever may be. BE PREPARED.

"Ideas come from all realities and timelines, they are always there, but it is the ability to tune in that has the potential of bringing them to life. So, prior to and during your adventures, focus is paramount as the essence of everything you do will have consequences through all eternity. If you are not alert in your empty mindedness, the journey you appear to have no control over can go either way.

"Which way depends on you. So, be clear of mind before you travel, because like meditation, when any thought creeps in, it can take over and evolve into something unexpected. If so, hopefully, the time will come when you realise 'this is not what was supposed to happen'."

As much as I was enjoying being in his company and learning from him, this was a lot of information for me to remember. I think he knew this because he shortly ended my lesson.

"Should you ever consider changing anything in the past timeline of your reality, you should know, it will no longer be your reality as it automatically becomes an alternate one, so there is no reason to do it. However, it has been known for the past to have been changed by future musings. There has to be passion and strong emotion for this to happen.

"Humanity doesn't believe this is possible, and I only tell you of this because it is not only rare, but also, only good can come of it. Should you chance upon any reality you feel happy in, it is unlikely your happiness will endure for any notable duration because you will not have the memories of that reality. And I mean every single one that made them the realities they are. You have to live yourself into your future. BREAK BOUNDARIES.

"We all have infinite futures shaped by the choices we make now. Now is eternal, so live it now."

As he finished, he took my right hand, cupped it with his one hand and covered it with the other, as he did, he said, "Time has come for you to return."

My ball began to spin faster and even without moving it, the force was apparent.

He didn't say it, but as he looked deep into my eyes, I felt his thoughts.

"Remember, be present. Be clear."

The next thing I knew, I was travelling through the electrified tube and back to my room._

THE UNION

Annie

For Araminter and I, it was different, in the sense we had no idea there were others like us.

I would always put my things away in the same place all the time, so whenever I needed anything, I always knew where to find them. My ball was always in my toy box at the top, but that night, for no particular reason, I took it to bed with me. I played with it before going to sleep, and this time there was no travel involved. I wasn't bothered as I was very tired and looking forward to going to sleep.

Once finished, I put it on my bedside table on its flat side, so it wouldn't fall off in the middle of the night and wake me.

I turned off my lamp and went to sleep.

I think it was three in the morning when I was gently awoken by a flickering light.

I was sleeping on my side with my back to my bedside table and as I turned to see where the light was coming from, my lamp began to pulse. One flash, then six, one again, then eight.

It did this repeatedly and even though I don't see well, it was starting to annoy me. I leant over to turn the lamp off but nothing happened. I flicked the switch a number of times and still nothing. I sat up to unplug it but it grew bright. Brighter than I had ever seen, and then it blew.

It wasn't quite complete darkness for me because as soon as the lamp went out, I noticed the red light from within the ball.

Wondering why the red light was on, I picked it up. The force was so overwhelming, I fell towards the floor. I don't remember hitting the floor because the darkness came.

I had travelled a lot over the last eighteen months, but I never met Araminter in any of my adventures since the Virtue toy store. Maybe this would be the time we'd meet again because I didn't initiate this journey. The ball was taking me.

Even though my arrival was instant, I distinctly remember a grey haze. There was obviously some kind of travel involved as my hair was always a few inches longer after each journey and lately, my parents had become curious at the speed my hair was growing.

The same as every other journey, I had no idea where I was.

This time, a toilet cubicle.

It could have been anywhere.

The lights were on, but not so bright that I couldn't see the three intense flashes of light that followed. First two, then a single one, accompanied by the sound of static discharge.

Since the adventure with Araminter in the VL machine at Virtue, the majority of my adventures since I had twenty-twenty vision.

The biggest shock I had this time, which I had never experienced in any other alternate reality, was my skin colour. I was black.

In the next cubicle, I heard girls talking about Brumalis.

Neither of them sounded like Araminter, but I knew they were something to do with me, because they were also talking about how they were black too and something about being bald.

I quietly unlocked the door to the cubicle and opened it just enough to see a boy stood by the mirror.

The two girls obviously heard the crack of electric too, and when they had finished talking, they opened their cubicle door. I came out of mine as they exited theirs, and one girl said the boy shouldn't be in here.

The girl with the orangey scalp noticed the ball in his hand and said he may be one of them to which I replied, "I think I am too."

We all held out our hands as we looked at each other.

Araminter

Since my adventure, I'd been having a recurring dream. More precisely, the same thing had been occurring in almost all of my dreams and I needed to find out what it meant.

It's very difficult to convey the feelings and emotions experienced in a dream. And I tried to explain it to my parents, but they didn't understand it either.

For the next week, I hadn't been right. I wasn't ill and there was nothing I could put my finger on. I just had no energy. Not even enough to play with my Brumalis.

It had been a long time since my adventure with Annie and I couldn't get it to take me anywhere since the last time I returned. Maybe it was because I dropped it from my window.

I probably shouldn't have but over a period of time, I showed the ball to the whole family, wondering if they would experience anything strange with it. If any of them experienced what I had, it most certainly wouldn't have been returned.

They all tried.

They enjoyed the experience of the force that came from it, and once they had it going properly, they competed for the highest score.

I watched intently, but there was nothing different, no wispy gold threads, flash or static discharge. Nothing at all.

Becoming despondent, everybody finished, so I took it back to my room where it stayed.

A week later, whilst I was sleeping, it happened again. The golden rat with an alarm clock chained around his neck appeared to me again, and every time he said, "Meet me at the Golden R at 10, 1 Ronic Alley."

It was looking me dead in the eye whilst pointing to the clock. I looked at the time. It struck ten and the alarm went off. This clock was different though. It wasn't with halves and quarters and numbered to twelve, it was segmented in thirds with no numbers but three words: Now, Now and Present. Now was placed where the ten and two would normally be and Present replaced the six. It had three hands. Two were pointing to Present and the other to where the ten would normally be. The fact that two hands were pointing to Present, I assumed it was ten o'clock rather than ten thirty.

Every time I looked at it, the same thing happened but this time the rat vibrated to the pulse of the alarm clock

I knew of Ronic Alley; it was on the way to the bazaar. It wasn't really an alley. It was a strange street in the fact that the way in was the only way out, and it was almost a suburb within itself as it spiralled around to the first building.

On one of my trips with Mum, she took a wrong turn. This annoyed her. She wasn't confident enough to perform a U-turn in the middle of this street so we had to continue to the end. She drove for a long time and when we eventually arrived, there was a very large building surrounded by empty space. It wasn't called the Golden R and there was no signage on it. To this day, I don't know what that building is. She drove around it and we made our way out.

I opened my eyes and saw the ball gradually vibrating itself towards the edge of the chest of drawers. The wheel was spinning so fast that when it eventually fell, it was speeding around the floor, banging into the walls and furniture.

Not wanting to wake anyone else, I quickly jumped out of bed to stop the noise. By this time, the lights were no longer flashing, but a constant red. I grabbed it and once again, through the tube I went.

I was nervous. It had been such a long time since the last adventure, I couldn't contain my excitement. I was hoping to see Annie again.

There was a difference though. This time, I was travelling towards a grey haze.

On opening my eyes after travelling through it, I was stood in an aisle full of toys. I looked ahead of me and also behind. There was no one.

The music playing in the store was audible, but not so loud I couldn't hear people in other aisles, accompanied by the occasional shouting over the screaming and crying children.

With my hands in my pockets, I wandered up and down this aisle just looking. On the top shelf, and out of my reach, there were balls that looked like mine. The boxes read, "Spin Ball Luminaries" and at the bottom of the box, in mostly gold letters, it read, "Made by THRilluminatiNG TOYS". Curious as to whether it had the same qualities as mine, I began to climb up the shelving.

The surprise of noticing the colour of my hands made me lose my grip. I fell to the floor and banged my head quite severely.

My skin is olive and, even in the height of summer, I never got this black.

Claudia

We went to see Dad at the care home and, after our visit, Mum had been on my mind quite a bit.

That same day, after returning home, Amelia found an injured bird in the garden. She brought it inside and insisted Mum searched the internet to find out how to care for a bird with a broken wing. She was a real carer. Always looking for something or someone to care for.

Mum found the information for her and Amelia was very caring towards it. She would even go into the garden to find food for it.

Once it was well enough, she released it, and I thought, *I wish she would have been old enough to have helped Mum and Dad at the time of the accident*, because I felt she was a born healer.

We went to bed that night and competed as usual, but as she hadn't been well for a few days, we only did it once. With our Brumalis placed on the tallboy between both our beds, we snuggled in and went to sleep.

I dreamt of Mum all night.

It was sad, but also nice, bittersweet almost. I never wanted it to end, but our slumber was interrupted. We were woken by two loud thuds as both Brumalis fell to the floor.

Faced with both balls flashing blue and red, I opened my eyes. From outside, our window must have looked like the emergency services were in the room.

I got out of bed and grabbed them both as quickly as I could. Last time, there was one gold wisp coming from each, but this time there were six. As the lights changed to a constant red, the six golden wisps on each ball combined, then from the inner wheel, they began to spiral towards each other.

I looked at Amelia. Excited, I gave her her ball.

The spirals joined and darkness came. It wasn't the same as last time though. The tube was similar, but the static wasn't arcing randomly as before, but more of a spiral around the outside of the tube.

The resistance was causing our hair to twist behind us and the opposite twist of both sides of Amelia's made it look like a fishtail plait. The first time we encountered the hair pulling, our first thoughts were it would be ripped from our heads, but with each journey it only ever grew, so although those thoughts were always in the back of our minds, we were used to the tension so thought nothing else of it as we hurtled through.

From a distance, straight ahead of us, looked like a solid dead end. I thought we were going to crash straight into it, but as we got closer, it was only a thick grey haze. Travelling through, our eyes were closed. We both suffered a sudden transitory head pain.

When we opened our eyes, we were stood in a cubicle in a ladies' toilet, which we later found out was in a Target store. The real shocker though was, as we looked at each other, we were both black. And bald! And when we spoke, we had different accents.

I saw myself in the mirror on the back of the door and apart from our baldness, we looked beautiful.

I wondered what this adventure was going to bring.

Amelia

I hadn't been well at all and I really didn't feel like I had the energy for this adventure with Claudia. Reluctantly, I took her hand and we were off.

Our journey began and the lethargy I was feeling left in an instant. I felt fine again. With this new burst of energy, I was now looking forward to our adventure. I was worried about the grey haze ahead of us as we hadn't encountered this before.

Exiting the haze, we found ourselves in a toilet cubicle and the surprise of being aboriginal was somewhat overwhelming.

We were excited about one of our superficial differences, but I was also worried about how we would be treated because of them.

Even though we were very young, we knew what harsh treatment the aboriginal people were subjected to and we were about to experience it first hand from a security guard at the store. But it was good for us. Even the limited insight to their treatment that day made us more compassionate towards them, probably more than most.

After our surprise, there was a flash and crack from the other side of the door. We opened it and saw a boy stood at the mirror admiring himself.

Firmly, I told him he shouldn't be in here, then Claudia noticed the Brumalis.

On realising he may be one of us, a girl appeared from the cubicle next to us saying she was one of us too.

This adventure was getting stranger by the minute.

Phreya

Since my first adventure, I felt so much better within myself and my time at school got a little easier to deal with. I now had hope about my sexuality.

The comments and snide remarks from the other children continued and still upset me, but I knew they didn't understand. I was beginning to care far less than I used to and I could now deal with them in a more accepting manner.

Mrs Osbourne commented on how different I was as she noticed I had been far happier lately. This was down to my solo adventures, one of which I thought I would never get home from.

Because school was unbearable most of the time, journeying to alternate realities was my only escape. It wasn't every day, but depending on how much fun I had, and how long I was there, I would sometimes go twice a night and even though nobody, including me, could see my Brumalis, I was willing to take the risk.

On every adventure, a tall slim middle-aged woman with a cap and dark glasses, always wearing the same clothes, eventually turned up. Able to see and touch the ball, she always helped me.

Artemis' acceptance of me without question was one reason I adventured alone, but the main reason was, more often than not, I was a boy outside of this reality.

I learnt so much when I travelled and that's why I've become more accepting of others and, more importantly, I established to myself that I am not the freak everyone said I was.

I didn't intend to journey that night, but my ball had been weird all day with cracking noises and random flashes. It wouldn't stop.

Mum and Dad eventually told me to put it in a box or put it in the garage as it was getting on their nerves. They couldn't stop it either.

It was my bedtime and I was tired anyway, so I kissed them goodnight and made my way to bed.

I intended to wrap it in a sweater and put it in the middle of my box of soft toys. I placed it on the bed, picked out one of my older sweaters from the drawer and sat back on the bed ready to wrap it.

The lights pulsed quickly, repeatedly flashing in a sequence. Curious, I began to count them. One blue, six red, one blue, eight red.

It did this constantly and once I realised the same numbers were repeating, it remained a constant red, which I thought odd, so I picked it up.

Whoosh! I was off again.

This journey was similar to some of the tube time I'd had with a haze ahead of me, and this time it was grey. I knew I was going to learn something on this one.

I opened my eyes.

"Shit."

I almost choked with the shock.

I was in a ladies' toilet stood in front of a mirror.

I was black.

Staring closely and feeling my skin, I noticed how smooth and blemish free it was. I liked this very much. Being black made me feel good!

As on every other journey, I grabbed my crotch to check my gender, just so my behaviour was correct and didn't raise suspicion.

|As I stood admiring myself in the mirror, three girls emerged from two of the cubicles behind me.

One of the bald girls said, "You shouldn't be in here. You're a boy!"

She sounded like Artemis with her accent and she looked a little like her too, except for the hair, or lack of it.

I stepped back and looked at myself. I was indeed a boy. I had on board shorts, flip flops and a T-shirt that showed off what were surprisingly large muscles for a child of my age.

The other of the two girls attempted a whisper. "Be quiet, Millie. I think he's one of us."

Another girl appeared from a cubicle saying, "I think I am too."

I turned around and, with my hand held out, they all looked and did the same. Which I think would have looked a bit odd to anyone walking in seeing three girls and a boy stood in the middle of a restroom all holding out their empty hands.

We stood in silence.

I was looking at them then at the Brumalis, assuming these were some of the others I had been searching for, for so long. By the looks on their faces, I wondered if they had been searching too.

The silence was broken by two girls barging in through the door.

We all swiftly put our hands behind our backs.

They came towards the mirror, the blonde girl with her head down. I noticed it was bleeding and the hair at the back of her head was red with blood.

On seeing this, the bald girl with the very red scalp rushed over and took control of the situation.

Crystal

My ball was different tonight.

Whether anyone else would have been able to see or feel it, I'm not sure, but the energy radiating, I had never felt before. Although I was in bed with my eyes closed, I could see a gentle pulsating light. I leant over to pick it up.

The light stopped, but now I could see light from the radiating energy. As I studied it, six thin wisps of smoky gold light began to emerge. Dancing gently up and down as they encircled my head, they made their way over to the mandala on the facing wall. The pulsating light charged luminous paint and the crisp clear geometry almost lit the room.

Once again, as before, it was like the mandala came alive. Only this time, instead of interpreting them as arcs, I saw three Cs, and immediately three things just came into my head: chakra, characteristics of living and colour. I knew these would be important to me because of the word games I regularly played with Mum.

The mandala was still moving as before. I then noticed, as I looked through the energy of the ball, the lights were a constant red.

My journey began.

The tunnel was statically charged, but this time it wasn't random. It was organised and spiralling around its inner surface.

After enduring the pulling on my hair, I finally entered a grey haze and though breathing was difficult, it didn't last long.

I opened my eyes and found myself surrounded by clothing. Within the clothing rail, everything hanging on it was multi-coloured and made of a very light and almost flyaway material. Even the slightest disruption to the surrounding airflow made these garments billow.

That was what was making my breathing difficult. I raised my hands to part the clothes; that was when I noticed my skin. My hands were black and, as I rolled up my sleeves, my arms were too.

Pulling myself from the floor and out from amongst the clothes, I wandered the shop in search of a mirror to see if I was completely black. I guessed I would be, but I wanted to be sure.

I turned to walk down one of the aisles and saw another girl. I didn't know if she was unconscious, but she was lying motionless with small boxes scattered around her.

As I got closer, she lifted her head. There was a lot of blood matted in her blonde hair. It looked like it had glitter in it too, but as I looked closer, her hair appeared almost fluid, causing the light to glint and appear like glitter from a distance.

I knelt beside her.

"What happened to you?" I asked.

"I don't know. I was climbing up the shelves to get a ball and noticed the skin on my hands was black. I'm not normally this black. That's when I lost my grip and fell."

"Are you hurt?"

"My head hurts a bit."

"Your head's been bleeding. Let's go to the toilets to clean you up," I said.

I helped her up, and noticed what was in the boxes strewn across the floor. They were balls like mine.

"What's your name?" I asked.

"Araminter. What's yours?"

"Crystal. I don't really like it, but I was named after a storm."

Her eyes lit up. "Really?" she replied.

"Yes. Why?"

"I was named after a storm too, but it was a sandstorm."

Whilst telling me this, I noticed she had one of the balls in her hand and I asked her where the box was for it.

"You can see it?" she questioned.

At that moment, I realised she was one of the seven, and the way she stared at me, I could tell she realised something too.

"Let's get you cleaned up," I said.

We made our way to the toilets and as we rushed through the door, there were three girls and a boy, and apart from the two bald girls, their hair was fluidly vivid as well.

The shorter girl had green hair and the boy's was blue. The other two girls were bald and the scalp of the taller one was a deep red. It looked as if the blood was about to seep from the pores, almost like she'd suffered a bad burn. The other girl's head was similar but lighter, like a gingery orange.

Acting very oddly, they quickly put their hands behind their backs. Instinctively, I knew what they were hiding.

We continued over to the sinks to clean up Araminter's head, when one of the girls rushed over to help. She washed the blood from Araminter's hair and saw the very small cut. She told Araminter her injury was minor and she would be fine.

Once cleaned up, she lifted her head. To my surprise, one of the other girls questioningly asked, "Araminter?"

She turned and, in the same tone, said, "Annie?"

I caught a glimpse of myself in the mirror and oddly, my hair was a different colour too. It was a purpley violet with the fluid quality of Araminter's, whose was a yellowish blonde.

Claudia, Amelia, Phreya and myself knew there were supposed to be seven, and Phreya and I were wondering where Artemis was.

After their curious look when we mentioned Artemis, we explained to Annie and Araminter, altogether we should be seven, and because this was the first time six of us were in the same place, we believed Artemis should be here too.

We left the toilets as a group and wandered the store. Talking and not paying much attention to anything, we were halted by a uniformed man wearing a cowboy hat. His uniform was a dirty brown with a silver embroidered name. It stood starkly in our faces.

Ian M. Bude

Store Security

Only then did we know he was a security guard. His dominating figure and stance stopped us in our tracks. He stood there with an expectant look on his face along with a very dark and thorny crown of thoughts. I knew this wasn't going to go well.

"And what do you think you're doing?" he said with a very stern look on his face.

We were all a bit scared, but I told him we were looking for our friend.

"Lost one of your mob, have you?"

I looked at him confused. I was unsure what he meant by this.

As he was waiting for me to answer, he looked at my hand then at Araminter's, then Phreya's.

"All of you, hold out your hands!" he shouted.

As we did, he said, "Bloody thieves all of you. Just can't be trusted."

It was at this moment Claudia realised what her characteristic of living was. She was the sensitive one and as the security guard very rudely told her to shut up, she cried even more, which brought Amelia's dominant chakra to the fore.

She assured Claudia everything would be okay and she would keep her safe.

It was getting weirder by the minute.

183

Amelia

The security guard could see our balls.

Aware they were an item sold in the shop, it didn't register with him that they may be what he had been searching for.

Unaware if any of the others had been made aware our Brumalis were inter-dimensionally sought, Claudia and I looked at each other when he mentioned them.

We were curious because he could see them, but unlike Pneuma, he couldn't touch them.

If this was the man Pneuma warned us of, we couldn't let him see the curiosity our faces displayed.

Crystal

He tried to take the balls from us, but every time he tried, his hand went straight through them as if they were just light. Looking confused, he couldn't work it out. Then in his frustration and anger, he clicked his fingers and pointed to our wrists. Six pairs of handcuffs appeared.

We were cuffed together in a line and the remaining single cuff he put on his right hand as he began to march us to the security office.

Being dragged through the aisles, Phreya said, "Is that Artemis?"

I looked over. Looking quite happy, and about to unwrap a lolly, she was stood with who I presumed was her mother, but she looked younger than I remembered her.

The security guard looked to where Phreya was pointing and saw Artemis unwrapping and about to eat a lolly. He sped up in her direction and pulled us all off our feet, dragging us in the process.

As he got to her, he grabbed her hand with such force, he broke her forearm.

I looked around and as people began to gather, we were almost surrounded by people holding their mobile phones, filming the events as they unfolded. Talking amongst themselves, they said how wrong it was that this little girl stole a lolly and blamed the mother for allowing and encouraging it. Then their attention turned to the six of us.

They speculated as they stared, assuming we had done something bad because we were all handcuffed together.

It was very emotional for us and by this time, we were all crying. We had just witnessed a grown man break a child's arm and the onlookers, for some reason, believed it was the child's fault. All of them but one.

Through the crowd, I saw a tall woman with a cap and large dark glasses. She stood with her head down and fists clenched. The debacle didn't seem to be bothering her and with great concentration on what we could see of her face, she appeared very focused.

I could feel my emotions emanating from the pit of my stomach throughout my whole body. We wanted to get out of here. We knew it was an alternate reality, but wanted to leave all the same.

My ball started to vibrate in my hand, then the energy from it was apparent to everyone.

As I held my ball out, the other girls and Phreya did the same. Six wispy golden threads emerged. They spiralled towards each other and as they combined into one, it shot straight up. It made contact with the ceiling of the store and a deep purple vortex opened.

Still handcuffed together, all in a row, we had a rapid ascent.

The last thing I observed before travelling along the tube with tears still falling was her smile gleaming white with a twinkle and a ping.

Artemis

Ⅰ was swimming, skimming stones, making dot pictures in the dirt, and generally enjoying the peace at the billabong, when the silence was broken.

I forgot about the tour group that was due. They were still quite a distance away, so I went to my usual place behind the rocks. I would normally stay there until they had gone.

I had my ball and while sat in the shade, I was spinning it to pass the time. While I was daydreaming about what Gambu had told me, I had an urge to peek around the rock.

Today's group was larger than normal. I watched as Uncle told them the usual stories when a man at the back of the group turned and stared directly at me. A tall man wearing an Akubra hat. I stared closely to make out his features then I quickly jumped back behind the rocks.

His resemblance to the security guard that grabbed my arm back at the store when I was younger brought back the memories of that day. I wasn't sure if it was him but my heart began to pound.

I looked again and he was still staring in my direction. Now I was beginning to get scared. I knew I was being irrational but I had to get away from here.

The rocks weren't quite as tall as me, so I stood with my back hunched over and began to run to the nearest trees in the opposite direction to the group.

I don't think he saw me.

With my stomach twisting in knots, I sat under one of the many boab trees. Ball still spinning, I continued to gently motion it with my wrist to calm myself. I was trying to get him out of my mind and I eventually did by thinking of Crystal and Phreya, and wondering who the other four would be.

Once calm, I thought I was clear minded, then in a split second, everything around me retreated at speed. I could see nothing in the blackness of the void, but I was okay. The appearance of the man in the Akubra scared me more.

Before I had the chance to form any meaningful thoughts, my surroundings returned as quickly as they disappeared. It was obvious to me this was an alternate reality because as the trees, rocks and even the billabong stopped so suddenly, they had a distinct jelly-like wobble to them.

I didn't realise it at the time, but by thinking of us all together while using the ball, I was attracting the others to me.

They all arrived.

They were very different to the last time I met them. Phreya and Crystal looked like they could have been my brother and sister, and when I saw the others, I thought, *Wow! All aboriginal kids. We're gonna change the world together.* This brought a smile to my face.

Then I looked closer. They had all been crying and were handcuffed together.

Once we'd all introduced ourselves, and I did what I could remember of the Welcome to Country, Crystal asked me about the security guard at the store.

I was about to ask her how she knew of that, but then I wondered whether or not I had mentioned it to her when we met before.

After trying to recall our first meeting, I told her what had happened at the store and that I saw someone very similar to him today.

She then asked, "Why is it that we came to you together?"

I then told her of Gambu and what he told me about having a clear mind and clarity in my thinking.

No sooner had I finished, they simultaneously said, "Ah!"

We all realised what happened.

We talked for a long time, until way after sunset. The full moon rose and still handcuffed, we eventually fell asleep.

Most of us woke very early. Probably three in the morning and I'm not sure who, but one of the others was talking in their sleep.

"Join the light! Join the light!"

It didn't sound like it was coming from Claud or Millie, so it must have been Phreya, because the voice was slightly deeper than the others. The four of us were laughing quietly as we wondered what he was dreaming about.

Araminter

We had a good rest and awoke to find ourselves distanced from each other. We noticed the handcuffs were gone but it was evident they were still there due to an occasional resistant unseen tug. Our recuperation had energised us and it would seem our Brumalis were energised too. They began with a pulsing vibration which grew more constant as the remaining three woke up.

None of us were motioning our hands to make the ball spin but it was exerting a force of attraction. Attraction towards Arty.

They moved closer and the lights from Arty's Brumalis began to glow. From a dim beginning, they grew brighter the closer we got.

The vibration woke Amelia, Claudia and Phreya and they were being pulled towards Arty and not wanting to be dragged, they rose to their feet.

The force was strong and initially we resisted, but realising it wasn't going to stop, we relaxed and went with it.

All looking at Arty, we wondered if she was calling us again, but the look on her face showed she was as confused as we were.

The blue and red of her ball were now spinning so fast, they merged as one, producing a beautiful deep dark purple aura which was gradually increasing and growing to surround Arty.

Getting closer still, we were becoming enveloped in the light. Stood evenly spaced around Arty, Phreya completed the circle.

From a constant, each Brumalis vibrated and lights pulsed randomly, or so we thought.

With Arty at the centre, Amelia's was first, followed by Claudia, then mine. Annie's and Phreya's followed, leaving Crystal's last.

Arty's ball pulsed in synchronicity with each of ours, eventually emanating a circular rainbow light similar to the one I witnessed around the VANTABLACK machine in Virtue, and the very same divine presence accompanied the thought.

When I made that connection, the encircling rainbow force exploded away from us causing a ripple.

A blinding beam of white light shot in both directions from the top and bottom of Arty's ball sending another six smaller beams to the centre of each of our foreheads. The pain wasn't intense but more of an ache, and with it came a tremendous influx of knowledge and information. With fear of my head exploding, for a moment we knew everything, but it was just for a moment.

As we looked at each other, there was a distinct look of embarrassment on Phreya's face. It bothered me and as I noticed the look on the faces of the others, they too seemed curious. I don't know what it was, but we all seemed to have been left with the essence of something that was personal to one of us and by the look on his face, I thought it was Phreya's and assumed it was a secret.

Artemis

Looking in both directions of the light, there was no end to it, no top or bottom. Even though we were stood, there was nothing below us. We were suspended in space.

Still looking below, a familiar sight was beginning to take form. It was Uluru.

I don't know if it was raising up or we were lowering down, but we were getting closer. Moving towards it, the others were trying to figure out what was down there.

Phreya said it looked like her school, Claudia said she couldn't see anything, Araminter thought it was a pyramid.

Listening to this, I wondered if we were looking at the same thing.

I said to Amelia, "What does it look like to you?"

"Nothing I have ever seen before," she replied.

Annie piped up. "All of you have always been able to see, but it seems you are all blind now! Can't you see it's a big top?"

Crystal hadn't said a thing.

After we shared our thoughts, we turned to Crystal. She had a knowing look about her.

She said, "It's not about what it looks like, that is just familiarity for us. It's about why we are here. This is going to be our place of learning."

Once settled on the rock and silent, we stared. I saw a figure stood alone and immediately, I knew it was Gambu. I thought how good it would be for the others to experience the Welcome to Country from an elder and hear his wisdom.

After his welcome, he began.

With all that's happened to us, we were eager to learn whatever it was we were going to be taught.

Annie

I couldn't believe it. No one could see it was a circus tent.

As we got closer, the top of the tent opened like a lotus flower. Inside the circus ring below were seven chairs and a purple backed platform in front of them; the now invisible handcuffs becoming more apparent with an intermittent pain.

We floated down all in a line, directly above the chairs. We were placed in our seats, then seven desks appeared in front of us. We waited. It was very quiet for what seemed to be quite a while, so we began to talk amongst ourselves.

There was definite movement in the air. It was a very slow vibration that gradually increased until I could hear it. Then Pockets, my brother's favourite toy clown, appeared in front of me.

The moment of the apparition, I heard Araminter laugh, and as I looked down the line, Crystal, Amelia, Phreya and Artemis were smiling, but Claudia had tears in her eyes. They didn't look like they were tears of upset or fear, but more of gratitude as she had a beaming smile on her face, then she said, "Mum?"

Araminter

Below me was the Great Pyramid of Giza.

From the height I was at, I thought I may have been able to see my house, but the pyramid was the only thing in sight and as we got lower, the sides began to move. From the point, all four sides started to open outwards and it looked like one big square with another square in the centre of it. The corners of the inner square were dead centre of the sides of the outer one.

The lower I was getting, the more walls were opening outwards and by the time it had stopped it looked like a flower. From my viewpoint, it looked really pretty. Sacred almost.

Once the walls finished opening, it exposed the centre of the pyramid and though it was supposed to be a burial chamber, it was more like an auditorium. There was a large segment of stepped seating facing towards what I think should have been a desk, but instead our focal point was a large cage almost half full with hay or straw surrounded by a number of items. We ended up in the front row.

Wondering what this was all about, I looked at the others and, like me, they had a look of confusion on their faces.

The straw began to move. Then it appeared.

Amelia

Everyone seemed to have a look of amazement on their faces as we drew closer to the ground. I was looking in the same direction, but I couldn't make out what it was I was seeing. It was a roof but I couldn't tell what the building was. Maybe it was because I was above it, but I couldn't understand why everyone was in awe of it.

We came closer and I could see it in all its glory. It looked like the building Pneuma described when Claudia and I had our first inter-dimensional trip.

The building was enormous. If this really was the mausoleum, I considered the number of corpses.

It had four sides made of the most highly polished marble I had ever seen. It had sculptures between each of the columns on all sides, which were holding up a pyramid-shaped roof, and just below the capstone was the most beautiful life-size chariot with horses. The whole thing appeared to be made up of many stones, but it was in fact one great stone.

When our feet touched the ground, I stared at this monolith and understood the awe the others held. As we stared, the statues came out of their poses and motioned us forwards. Which we did.

Now close to the large marble wall, a hole appeared at its centre and began to grow. When it stopped, it edged itself with gold creating a ring.

Starting at the top and following the circle, another six appeared, and it kept duplicating this until the wall was covered. Everywhere I looked, I could see flowers on this wall. It was one and it was many.

After admiring this for a while, the circles began to disappear, one by one, in a spiral. The flowers gradually faded, taking the wall with it, until the whole wall had gone.

I noticed the statues that were between the columns were now surrounding us to the sides and back. We looked at them as they began to slide slowly towards us. There was a force moving us forwards too. It moved us to the centre of the tomb where seven beds were arranged in a large circle. Each at the side of a bed, we sat as the statues formed a larger circle around us.

Just back from the middle of the floor and at the centre of the beds, hovering just above our head height, was an intense purple light backed by an upright large spinning white disc. Though the ceiling was solid, the light shone through to the sky, which was the blackest black and peppered with stars.

I thought it was as bit strange because prior to entering the tomb, it was daylight. Everything went dark and the only light was coming from the purple beam.

What looked like a thick flurry of snow began to fall from the bottom of the light. We stared as it began to take form.

In front of us, Pneuma appeared.

Claudia

We were having such fun speculating on Crystal's comments. Phreya said maybe we were going to learn how to become wizardesses. That started everyone off imagining all the amazing things we would be able to do.

Then the light came and everything disappeared; we were suspended in space. The others were looking to see what the light was shining on, but what I saw was nothing but blackness and rain, although I wasn't getting wet.

They were describing different things, but as there was nothing there for me, I looked to the light. Shining through the raindrops, a flower of multi-coloured light formed. It was very pretty.

Within the light, the formation of a building was beginning to appear. I stared in wonder. The red roof looked familiar. The front windows were already in place as the door grew between them. It was Dad's house. The flower filled front garden was completed with the lemon tree on the left.

Raising as it got closer, the floor opened up. It was strange looking up into the house but the views of the furniture Mum chose, along with her Art Deco decor, statues and artwork gave me comfort.

It landed around me and in front of me, Mum appeared.

I was numb with happiness and gratitude. She knew that was why I was crying.

Phreya

I don't know why everyone looked so amazed by my school. There was nothing mystical about it. In fact, I would say it was no different to any other and quite boring as far as schools go.

As it got closer, I could see my classroom. Through the finely painted yellow flower on the window, I could see the teacher's desk at the front as usual, and the only other furniture in there was seven chairs equally spaced around it. Which, under the circumstances, I don't suppose was odd at all.

I saw Mrs Osbourne, beautiful as always, but this time she had a shimmer about her I hadn't noticed before. She turned her head to look out of the window, and when we made eye contact, all seven of us were pulled towards her as if we were being sucked though the tube of an invisible vacuum.

We were headed straight for the square steel-framed window.

I thought to myself, *none of the glass will survive this.* I think we were all expecting some cuts and pain going through it.

On the approach, we closed our eyes, waiting for the sound of breaking glass.

Nothing.

Time slowed as we passed through the window into the classroom. Without pain or breakage, we became the window frame and the glass.

Once in the classroom, the handcuffs were gone. The six of us began to hold our wrists, one at a time in either hand, and twist them gently. They were sore by this time.

We looked at Mrs Osbourne as she continued to stare towards the window. We turned to see what she was looking at and there they were. Two sets of handcuffs were encased in the four central pieces of glass. A cuff in each pane with the small chain overlapping the window frame. The cuffs of the left were open and looked like a number one; on the right, the cuffs were closed. They looked like the number eight.

The other five sets were open and formed a circle around this number. I counted the panes of glass.

"There are sixteen windows," I said.

This outburst triggered a memory in us all.

We looked at each other questioningly thinking, *What does this mean?*

These four numbers were popping up all the time, seemingly out of nowhere and always in the same order. I'd seen them a lot in my solo adventures, but only now was I thinking they had meaning. Maybe it was because we were now all together? Maybe it had a meaning for all of us? Was this what we were going to learn?

We turned to Mrs Osbourne and, with a smile on her face, she motioned for us all to sit.

Crystal

S at with the others, I sensed this would be an unforgettable experience. Everything they were seeing was a projection of their individual minds. People they knew, places they had been and everything that would make their experience believable to them.

The energy coalesced to make it individually relevant.

They assumed they were seeing the same thing and couldn't really understand why each other's reactions were different. For me, it was different. I saw it for what it was. Energy. All around me was energy. To my right were six balls of energy. I was no longer a body, but a ball of energy too.

Directly in front of me was one large ball of infinite energy that looked like a sun, but I could see no edge to it. Though I saw it in front of me, it enveloped me. It appeared to occupy all space and time.

From the feeling I had within, I knew this was our source and judging by the reactions of the others, it seemed I was the only one aware of its natural state.

I felt Araminter's pyramid, Amelia's mausoleum and Phreya's school. I felt them all appear separately and simultaneously, including Claudia's house, Annie's big top and Uluru for Arty.

Observing them all within the energy I was, and though Araminter's rat amused me, the whole thing was a surreal, yet divine experience.

I was everything in that moment.

We were now ready to learn.

Artemis

As I looked at the other six, I think they were as excited as me. We were staring at Gambu in anticipation of what was to come, except for Claudia who still had tears in her eyes and Amelia who was looking all around her.

This was going to be a turning point for us.

When I heard him speak, he had my complete attention. Though today, he had the manner of a schoolteacher, I could still feel that all-knowing, all-encompassing, all-loving essence of him.

"So many students ready at the same time," he began. "And from so many places throughout the universe. We believe we are all going to enjoy our short time together. Settle in and make yourselves comfortable. There will be a lot of information today."

When he said, "So many students", I thought he meant just the seven of us, but as I turned again, the top of Uluru behind me was full of other beings.

"Hello Artemis. I see you succeeded in getting the others to you. It is good the seven are together. There is a lot we have to teach and a lot you have to learn, and it is not just by listening that you will understand. You will also feel all that we share. So, if you are ready, we will begin."

My anticipation was at its peak. I was hoping to learn how our balls worked along with instruction on how to make our travels as safe as they could be.

"You all have great opportunities ahead of you and whatever your dreams are for your life, your journeys are of utmost importance for achievement of them, so accept all that comes your way and be happy in everything you do. Enjoy it.

"Your birthplace has a bearing on how you view your life and others. This will shape your experiences. Life is not just about your body and the things you do. Most importantly it's about how you think, but there are other things vital to your lives too.

"Your chakras, your characteristics of living and deadly sins. Your dominant traits of these groups may clash with each other and should this happen, you have to learn how to deal with those which don't serve you.

"There are other things you will learn of today which will be of great help throughout your lives, so pay attention to everything. Everything we share today is not just for the seven of you. It is for all.

"You may think some things aren't relevant to you as individuals, but know this, our message is not in our words, but our vibration. Over recent times, there are things that have presented themselves to you on many occasions, which some of you have noticed and some have not. The most persistent are numbers, and today, we shall begin with seven.

"On the Earth Plane, there are many beliefs in things which humanity has grouped by seven, so seven parts make one collaborative group. Of all these groups, there are five which relate to you all personally. The other two came into being when you were born. The first is you all as a group, and the second is your diffabilities."

When he said "diffabilities", I thought he meant disabilities. I looked behind me then down the line at the other six and I wasn't aware any of us had disabilities, apart from Annie's blindness, but even that was only a disability from our perspective. It didn't seem to hinder her life.

Gambu must have noticed the confusion on my face as this was explained when he continued.

"There is no such thing as a disability. We say diffability because we know you are all different and possess different abilities."

He paused as we began to comprehend what he had said.

"It was your desire before you left the non-physical. And now it has come to pass, we can start to process the reason you chose your planet. We will tell you what we know will help you, but you have to find out many things for yourselves because, as you will find throughout your lives, anything you do for yourself will inevitably be of more value to you, than if things are done for you.

"So, listen carefully and feel that which we are. You have every aspect of every group within you, yet you each have a dominant aspect of each group, and when you become aware of these, that is when the force of your combined power will be at its greatest.

"As a group, you are the same, yet very different, and as a group 'The Diffability Girls' describes you perfectly. Some of you have used your abilities already, though you are not aware of them as abilities, and Araminter unknowingly has used her ability on two occasions already.

"There are so many abilities and so many ways in which they can be used. They will be very useful during your adventures together, but timing is important too. You can have all the power and all abilities possible, but if the time isn't right, they will not be at your command. Now, can any of you think what your abilities may be?"

Annie straight away put up her hand. "The ability to give sight," she said.

He smiled and said, "Anyone else?"

We all looked at each other.

There was silence.

"Araminter, would you like to come to the front?"

She made her way to Gambu, smiling and looking back at us.

As she stood at his side, he said, "The ability to manifest sight is not yours, Annie. One of your abilities is the power of your senses.

"Over the years, your body has compensated for your lack of sight, so your hearing is more acute than most, as is your sense of taste, smell and touch. However, on your adventures, you can control this by increasing or decreasing the sensitivity of it to suit your surroundings and your needs."

I wondered why Araminter was with Gambu, when he turned to her and said, "Araminter. You are the Manifester. The day you were in Virtue, do you remember the shimmer on your fingers when you wiped away Annie's tears, and the same when you rubbed your hands when you were cold?"

"Yes," she said.

He turned to us and said, "Okay. Who's hungry?"

All the time we had been together, none of us had even thought about food, but as soon as he mentioned it, we all felt as if we hadn't eaten for days. I put up my hand and turned to see everyone else doing the same. I had no idea how he was going to feed everyone there.

He turned back to Araminter.

"What do we need to do?" he asked her.

"Get a lot of food!"

"Correct. Now, when the clown appeared to help you out of the VL machine, what were you thinking?"

With the look on her face, you could see she was reliving that experience.

"We wanted a way out of the virtual life."

"And why do you think it was the clown that helped you?"

She thought for a while and said, "Because of the clowns we noticed in the shop?"

"That's right, but it was mainly to do with Annie. They reminded her of Michael, which gave her comfort, and the feeling within her was so strong, as you rubbed your hands together, you manifested the clown.

"But it isn't just rubbing the hands and it isn't always immediate as you demonstrated with Annie's sight, but as you practice this, you will learn a lot more about this ability." He turned to everybody and said, "Right, if you all think of what it is you would like to eat, Araminter will serve you."

Everyone began to talk amongst themselves, suggesting different foods to each other.

Gambu reminded them, "You need to focus carefully on exactly what it is that you want. If you are not clear, you will be very surprised at what turns up in front of you."

There was silence again and Gambu was quietly saying something to Araminter.

She closed her eyes for a while, and as she opened them, Gambu gave her a nod. She began with some strange hand movements, clicking fingers and slapping her fist. The first time she did it, a red, white and green light shot from her fist. It hit the floor then flew up over my head and landed in the lap of an Indian boy.

"And what do you have, Akarsh?" Gambu asked.

He held up his plate and shouted, "Exactly what I wanted: Chicken Chettinad."

Gambu nodded to Araminter again. This time, three white lights came from her fist.

"Mai Ling?"

A Chinese girl stood up and said, "Rice, chicken and noodles."

Araminter did it again and it looked like the light was struggling to leave her hand. She looked at Gambu.

He smiled and said, "Just wait a moment, it will leave."

Eventually, the light shot out with immense pressure. It hit the ground with such force, it made a hole the size of a small animal. Then it arced directly above Crystal's head and landed in the lap of a Jamaican boy.

He screamed and as we looked around, he had a goat sat in his lap.

Everyone laughed at what had appeared.

"Okay. Everyone calm down. Kendrick, what did you want to eat?"

The goat jumped off his lap and Kendrick replied with a smile on his face, "Curry goat!"

Everyone laughed again.

Gambu said to us all, "You see. Clarity. Whatever your desire is, be focused. We, as your source, respond to the vibration you offer, and if your vibration isn't pure, you will receive a variation of your desire. As you saw with Kendrick, the essence of what he wanted was there, but he wasn't focused enough to get the meal he desired. So, think again and Araminter will oblige."

Araminter

When the creature stood to open the gate of the cage, it must have been about six feet tall. It was gold and there was a large clock around its neck which read ten o'clock.

It was the rat from my dreams.

The surprise at physically seeing something so funny made me laugh out loud, and I turned to my right and Annie was looking at me wondering what I was laughing at. I was surprised she didn't find it funny. In fact, no one else was laughing. Claudia was even crying, which I thought was very odd. Maybe she was afraid of rats?

The rat spoke. "Hello Araminter, it's good to see you again."

Again? I thought. Then I remembered. I followed a golden rat in Virtue when I found the shoelace.

"It's good to see the seven are one today. You can see from our surroundings, this is a place of learning, and we are here today to teach you what you need to know."

I was so excited about this. I mean, whoever heard of a talking rat!

"Hello everybody. Today I am Professor Pie. Welcome to your Intuit lesson."

As he said this, we heard a thunderous "Hello Professor Pie" from behind us.

We all turned to see who said this. The auditorium was packed, not an empty seat to be seen. There were far more children than adults, but there were also other beings. Some were like the aliens portrayed in books and films, some were jelly-like figures of constantly changing form, and some were like clouds of gas. There were a lot more, but I don't know how to describe them as I'd never seen anything like them before.

With no idea where they appeared from or who or what they were, I don't think any of us expected to be accompanied during our learning. In silence, we were looking at the different beings for such a long time, trying to take in all of the information about them.

"Ahem"

The rat coughed and regained our attention. He began by speaking about groups of seven and abilities we were yet to realise and how he would help us demonstrate those which we had already unknowingly used.

But also, he said, we would have to learn most for ourselves.

Then he called me. "Araminter, would you like to come to the front?"

I left my seat and made my way down, looking back and smiling at the others as I went.

"Would anyone like to guess the ability Araminter is going to perform for us today?"

I don't know if it was the colour of my hair or the fact the rat was gold, but most thought I was going to turn things into gold.

Some said, "Change into an animal."

A few said, "Make something disappear."

He turned to me and asked the same question.

From what everyone said, I replied, "Make something disappear."

He looked up at the class and said, "What can you tell me about magnets?"

"They attract metal," Phreya said.

"All metal?" the professor asked.

She paused for a while then said, "I think only metals that are similar to what the magnet is made of."

"That's a very important point, but we will cover that later. Anyone else?"

A cloud of gas emitted a vibration to the professor and all others present. I interpreted it.

"It has a positive end and a negative end. If you put two or more together, the positive and negative will always attract each other, yet still only have one positive and negative end, so in effect there are many different magnets but there is only one and they are always balanced."

Once this being finished vibrating its answer, the professor said, "Did all of you follow that?"

We all said, "Yes."

He continued. "Very comprehensive, Ohmlar. Thank you. The point I was trying to make was balance, and getting back to Araminter, if she was to make something disappear, how could we balance that?"

"Make something re-appear," Claudia said.

"Very good. Now who's hungry?"

Everybody put up their hands. The professor then told everyone to think about what they wanted.

While they were thinking, he said to me, "Do you remember the man at the bazaar when you were younger?"

I looked at him, trying to remember who he meant.

He smiled at me and, with his back to the others, he clicked his fingers on both hands then slapped a loose fist. Then I remembered. I turned around to face the girls and everyone else.

He said, "Close your eyes and imagine yourself doing that."

I hadn't done that for a while, but it didn't take long to get the hang of it again. I opened my eyes and he nodded to me. I did it once.

With a mild burning sensation in my hand, three lights shot out. They hit the floor first, then headed towards an Indian boy.

Though it was a light, it wasn't travelling at the speed of light. It was gradually making its way to the boy, attracting different energies on its way.

As it landed in his lap, he said what it was and I wondered if that was why my hand had a mild burn.

The next one went well, so I did it again.

On the third attempt, a goat landed in a boy's lap.

The professor said, "Vamoose," and the goat disappeared, then explained what just happened.

After a few moments of focus by everyone, I began again. I was slapping my fist so fast it looked like I had a Roman candle in my fist.

The rat then told me to open up my hands and spread my fingers. When I did this, there was continuous multi-coloured light flowing from each finger. It kept splitting until it was in the laps of everyone.

Once everyone had a meal, it stopped.

It didn't feel like I had any control over it, but I was told I did and I would come to understand and learn to control it with time.

The professor told me I could go back to my seat, and when I got there, there was a big bowl of kushari waiting for me.

He returned to his cage while we all ate.

Annie

Once we had eaten, Pockets returned, still in the clown outfit. "Okay, are we ready to continue?"

After what Araminter had just done, everyone was very keen.

"Right, who wants to be part of our next demonstration?"

I put up my hand.

He continued. "In her reality, Annie is almost blind." He looked at me and asked, "How do you normally read?"

"Braille," I said.

"And can you tell the others how that works?"

I explained. "When I feel the paper, there are raised dots. They relate to letters and numbers, and depending on which of the six dots are raised, I can tell what letters or numbers they are."

"Is there anything on your body that is similar to that?"

"No," I said.

He turned and picked up six balls and, as he began to juggle them, he said, "Think again."

I couldn't think of anything, so I said, "I don't think so."

He stopped juggling the balls and suspended them in the air in front of him in two vertical rows of three.

As I was staring at the balls, he changed the colour of them, trying to spell out a word to me.

He looked me square in the eye and said, "Ready?"

With no idea what he meant, I reluctantly said yes.

In the order he pointed to them, they came straight at me. They dissipated before they hit me, which was lucky because I never moved a muscle.

Suddenly, the moles on the side of my head began to throb. I started to rub them with my finger. Each throb had a different configuration. It was then I realised what Pockets did.

My moles were in the same configuration of the braille template and as I felt the moles throb, the word the clown sent me was, "this, this, this, this."

"Do you know what it is now?"

"Yes," I said.

He continued. "Every single one of you have abilities. Some are related to your birthmarks some are not. Annie is different to the rest of you in that way because she wasn't born where she was intended, so the storm missed her. As a consequence, her birthmark is different to the six of you, as she has moles rather than the faint imprint you all have.

"Nevertheless, it is still an ability that needs to be learnt. Now, does anyone else have anything similar to this?"

Amelia sheepishly put her hand up.

"And what do you think yours is, Amelia?"

"Well, it's only happened once, but I had a twitch I just couldn't stop."

"That is correct. At that time, we were attempting to prepare you for the news about Daigo and Holly. Yours is similar to Annie's, but instead of braille, yours is in Morse code, so learn this. Anyone else?"

Silence again.

"Okay then. So, as well as an avenue of communication with us, it is also a warning sign to you, so always pay attention to them. They may save your life one day."

Amelia

Once Pneuma had finished telling us about Annie's birthmark and my twitch, she finally came to me.

"Talking of saving lives brings me to Amelia. Amelia is different to the seven of you, but not in a way that is obvious. As I mentioned earlier, there are seven groups of seven that are a part of all of you, with one dominant aspect of seven that resonates strongly.

"We will tell you of your chakras and other groups of seven, but you will have to discover for yourselves which of each group is strongest. Some of you already know what some of the qualities and abilities are, but as we have said before, don't waste your time looking for them."

On hearing this, Phreya asked, "Why?"

"Well, how will you know you've found them if you don't know what it is you're looking for?" Pneuma replied. "We are constantly guiding you to their recognition, and this will continue until understanding is gained.

"Six of the seven dominant aspects within her are perfectly matched and this is why Amelia is currently the exception. Therefore, it is wise to travel with her at all times, as eventually, she will be able to cure all ills.

"We shall begin with the third group: chakras. These are your energy centres, which are part of the non-physical body within. These are very important to your wellbeing as this is one of the ways in which we flow through you. When they are not balanced, they cause a variety of problems for the body and mind, so it is important you understand them.

"Amelia's dominant chakra is the root, and it's from here she gets the instinct for survival and this is so strong within her she is unable to distinguish the difference between her need and the need of others.

"We know our connection with everything and everyone and it is her strong feeling of this connection through the root chakra that makes her feel the need of others."

Pneuma turned to me and said, "Do you recall the moment in the toilets when Araminter came in with her head covered in blood?"

I nodded.

"This was one of those moments when you can't not do what *you* know is right. It all comes from within. It is us, continually presenting an urge you cannot suppress."

Everything was beginning to make sense to me now. I was beginning to understand the feeling of uselessness that consumed me when I saw suffering and was unable to help and the feeling of joy when I could, like the bird in the garden I insisted on caring for and the time in the toilets when Crystal came in with Araminter and her blood-soaked matted hair.

"The fourth group is the characteristics of living. These are inherent in all sentient beings and as we know from what happened in the alternate reality of Artemis' memory, Claudia is the sensitive one.

"Can any of you tell me what you think the others may be? Before you answer, think of how your body works."

This was something I was going to really enjoy and while everyone was sat there thinking about their bodies, I turned to Pneuma and said, "Food, breathing and growing."

"Very good. Anyone else?"

Claudia shouted, "Feelings."

Artemis said, "Moving."

Phreya said, "Pooping."

Such a boys' answer.

Everyone laughed.

There was silence for a while and just as Pneuma was about to speak, Crystal said, "Reproduction."

Crystal had been very quiet throughout our lesson and I was wondering if she was enjoying it as much as everyone else seemed to be.

Pneuma continued. "Very good. So, we have nutrition, respiration, movement, excretion, growth, reproduction and, finally, sensitivity. You may not understand at this time but these seven aspects are fundamentally present in every living organism, including your planets. Now, what do you think Amelia's dominant characteristic is?"

We simultaneously said, "Respiration."

"Good. The link was obvious to you all."

As Pneuma said my root chakra was most dominant, I thought this was why I was always drawn to safety and survival. Whenever I recognised danger or when someone or something was hurt, I wanted to help every time. This desire to help made me realise my characteristics of living were perfect for me too.

Even though there were many groups to learn, it was always easy for us to find our own. It was always that which resonated most within each of us.

"The fifth group, I will leave for last, so, onto the sixth. You call it colour, we feel it as geometric light. The geometric light reflectofractor, or Newton's disc as it is called on your planet, has a property of almost complete invisibility. Can anyone tell me anything about that?"

I hadn't heard of this before, but Phreya seemed to know a lot about it and went on to explain it.

"When you shine white light through a prism, it splits into seven colours. One time at school, we had to make a disc and paint the seven colours of the rainbow on it. We made two small holes each side of the centre and then threaded some string through and tied it in a knot.

"In either hand, we held the string with the card in the middle, then made circular motions so the disc twisted the string, then we pulled the string. The card spun so fast all the colours blended together and disappeared, and the card was white until it slowed, then we could see all of the colours again."

"Very good, Phreya. So, like the colours on the disc, individually, you are one of seven, and like the colours, as a group, you are one made of seven.

"In essence, you are the individual but also the whole, and the whole is always greater than the sum of its parts. Would you all like to see a demonstration of this?"

Everyone said yes and I was keen too. I understood what she said but I couldn't visualise it.

She clapped her hands twice and the disc that had been spinning behind her for the whole lesson, stopped dead and we could see all the colours. She then began to blow on it, gently at first, but gradually faster.

Two things amazed me about this. The first was seeing all the colours blend then disappear to white, and secondly, she blew at the disc with just one breath for about thirty seconds and wasn't panting for breath afterwards.

She turned back to the class and continued to talk about colour.

"Now some of you will have noticed your hair has changed colour. Is there anything else different about your hair at this time?"

We all mentioned how the light seemed to pass through it.

"Yes. Now this only happens on the occasions when you will be travelling together. The reason for this is concealment and should you lose your hair during the process of travelling, the shimmer of your heads does the same.

"When you travel alone, you appear to travel in a straight line, and people that see you assume you are shooting stars. When you travel together as a group, you don't feel it but you are spinning too. Then you are assumed to be a UFO.

"Stories have been told of UFOs travelling through the sky and how they suddenly disappear. This is why. The circular speed becomes so fast, the reflectofractor properties of it blend with the background and they see it no more."

Pneuma lost everyone's attention as looks of incomprehension came over everyone as they imagined this.

"I think it's time for refreshments. Would any of you like something to drink before we continue?"

Everyone said yes please.

She turned to Araminter and said, "Would you oblige?"

Araminter stood up from her seat and, with both hands, started to make wave motions up and down, from her elbows to her fingertips. A sine wave of light emanated from them to everyone in the room, and in our laps appeared a container made of light but full of water.

"Getting the hang of it already. Well done," Pneuma said to her.

During our five minutes of refreshment, we discussed the lesson, then regaining the room's attention, Pneuma continued.

"The seven wonders of the ancient world. Not all remain, so I will show them to you as they were."

She asked Ohmlar to join her. All present of human form and most alien forms, who had never witnessed a being like this before, turned to see Ohmlar's gas formation swirl and expand to fill the entire space above us.

The presence I felt when Ohmlar was demonstrating was similar to how I felt around male members of my family and I interpreted Ohmlar as a masculine energy.

A being from Saturn, he had so many colours within, combined with an immense amount of arcing static. Ohmlar was a beautiful but curious sight.

As the gas cloud condensed above Pneuma's head, she held her hands up as if to grab this disc of gas. The attraction between Ohmlar's manifestation and Pneuma's hands was so strong, the disc of gas followed them as they lowered. Once it was directly in front of her and us, she took the stethoscope from around her neck and placed the two ends in her ears. The other end was dangling at the front of her lab coat facing outwards. It was odd for her to have such a modern device, but I was used to anomalies by then.

With her head facing down, she quietly spoke an enchantment and as she slowly lifted her head, a vortex began to appear from the stethoscope and Ohmlar was sucked in.

As more words left her lips, fingers began to appear at the centre of the stethoscope. There was someone within, trying to escape the tiny hole.

We stared.

The fingers became hands and grew bigger, enlarging the hole until we could no longer see Pneuma.

Then, he stepped out. In a booming voice, we heard, "I am the Colossus of Rhodes. Welcome to the old world."

I had never seen a man of this stature. I could see why he was called that.

He knelt down and put both hands palm down on the floor. Turning them outwards, he blew into the space between. From his mouth came a tirade of bricks and pillars.

He gradually moved his hands apart, whilst blowing from side to side and upwards at the same time. When he was stood again with his arms outstretched, there in front of us was the most magnificent temple with pillars all the way around.

With a slight brush of his hand, he moved it to one side as Pneuma's voice echoed, "The Temple of Artemis."

We thought this would resonate most with Artemis

The Colossus said, "Open."

All pillars at the front of the temple moved from the centre outwards, revealing a large statue.

It moved towards the opening as the temple shrunk into the background and disappeared. It was the statue of a man sat on what I guess was a throne, with his lower half draped in a gold material. His right hand held a statue of a lady.

Pneuma, now in sight, said, "The statue of Zeus."

He arose from his throne and stood facing the Colossus. Having power over the weather, Zeus manifested a storm. Thick black clouds with thunder, lightning and rain were suspended between them. They put their hands into it and out fell a replica of the building we were in and a pyramid.

"The Mausoleum of Halicarnassus and the Great Pyramid of Giza," Pneuma said.

Then a variety of plants and trees emerged, with colours as vivid and intense as the fragrance. Suspended in mid-air, gentle movement from an apparent breeze wafted the aroma throughout.

In my awe, I saw Phreya wipe her eyes as she commented how beautiful they were.

"The Hanging Gardens of Babylon."

With a flash, it all disappeared but the delicately intense fragrance lingered a while longer.

Zeus and the Colossus threw the storm into the ground and they followed it in. As they disappeared, a rumbling began. A volcano shape emerged from the ground but instead of the expected lava eruption, there was a pulsating white glow.

Staring in silence, it began to elevate.

From the bubbling lava grew a flame-topped building with fortifications on all sides. Though its purpose was obvious, I had never seen one like it before. The flame pulsed and with each intensity, it lit up each wonder in turn, eventually becoming encircled by them.

Pneuma continued. "These are the seven wonders of the ancient world. The last being the Lighthouse of Alexandria. Whoever this resonates with will become the beacon of your group, and with the assistance of Araminter, this beacon of light will show you the way. Amelia's is the Mausoleum at Halicarnassus, but what resonates with you?"

She turned to me and said, "As I told you on our first meeting, the birthmark you carry is resonant of the mausoleum but not about death. It is a place of recuperation, so with the help of Araminter, she will be able to manifest this safe haven. A place of recuperation for you all whenever necessary. Onto the deadly sins. This is the fifth group.

"These are so named as they have brought death to many, either from outside forces or internal conflict. They are envy, gluttony, greed, lust, pride, sloth and wrath."

We knew what all of these things meant, and we knew what we did and didn't want to have an affinity with.

"What do you think Amelia's is from this group?"

No one muttered a word and even I didn't know the answer to this one. I was surprised when she said sloth, but she went on to explain it was more observational than anything else, although if I was ever ill myself, I would suffer the lethargy of this more than most do because when I heal others, I absorb from them.

"Absorbing too much from others will limit your abilities, so we are going to show you how to release that energy to us. Amelia, would you like to come to the front?"

I marched up with such conviction. I wondered what I was going to learn about me.

"Lie down with your head at east."

She showed me the direction of east and as I began to lie down, she said to the others, "This works for all, so if you have any discord within, do this and you will feel better gradually until you master it. Face east if you are sat or stood or place your head at east if you are lying down."

As I lay waiting and ready to begin, she said, "Amelia. Close your eyes and visualise your body as pure non-physical energy."

I turned my head to look at her. She saw my confused look and explained.

"Whatever position you find yourself in, close your eyes and visualise that. As you focus on the body, see it made from pixels of light. As you do this, you will notice various colours making up your whole body. Wherever in your body you see any darkness, this is where the blockage of energy is residing, and the closer to black the colour appears, the more in need of cleansing you are."

This example of what that may look like was helpful but I was struggling to hold the vision of my body like that, and Pneuma was very intuitive.

She continued to say, "If you are unable to see your body as light, it is of little consequence. However, its presence in your mind's eye will work, and you will feel the blockages if you can't see them."

This put me at ease and I relaxed further as she began her instruction.

"Begin with your focus at the toes and really feel every part of them. Those without bodies, focus at your edges. From your toes and edges, gradually move your focus up through the whole of your body or inwards to your centres, feeling as you go.

"As you travel up or inwards, feel the energy differences. If there is any part of you that feels different, imagine forcing it up your body towards your throat or in from your edges to your centre.

"Don't forget to include your head in this cleansing as this is the source of all dark manifestation because, as we will learn, everything begins with thought. And those without bodies, include the part of you where you believe your mind resides.

"Once you have done this, visualise yourself looking at your form. Notice if there are any dark spots or clumps of energy left. If so, do it again and again until you can see a consistently clear field of energy.

"Once this is complete, you will have a dense energy in your throat chakra or obliquemvibra. When you get to this stage, it is important that you breathe in a circular motion with a long breath in through your nose and out through your mouth, but do it with force from your diaphragm.

"This will ensure everything leaves and as it is released from the throat chakra, this communicates to us and we will take it from you. A blocked throat chakra or obliquemvibra, as Ohmlar has, can affect the balance of all other chakras."

Pneuma continued the lesson and I was left to my cleansing until I felt my blockages had cleared. I got up and I felt so much better, which was strange because I didn't feel there was anything wrong with me prior to the exercise.

Pneuma thanked me for my participation and I went back to sit with the others.

Claudia

Mum looked so angelic and I was so happy it was her giving the lesson today. I wanted to go up to her and give her a hug, but I knew it wasn't the right thing to do at the time.

She demonstrated many things and shared so much information. I absorbed every word and movement since she appeared. I zoned out everything just so I could take in every minute detail. It was the best day of my life.

When she finished talking about belief, the atmosphere of the whole house changed. As I looked at everyone else, they looked like mannequins. Everything had stopped, even Ohmlar was still.

I looked at Mum. She smiled and called me to her. I had never felt such great emotion. There was so much love emanating; it was indescribable.

With gratitude and tears of joy streaming down my face, I left my seat and ran to her.

As we hugged, I felt we had merged to one. The power of her energy was felt in every cell of my being. At that moment, I knew everything about her.

The reason she went into a coma that day was because, on a spiritual level, that was when she chose to make a partial transition. It was nothing to do with me or Dad. It was her choice and she knew she would do far greater good for me as a guide rather than a mother. Though I understood this, a small part of me still wanted her home. Not just for me, but for Dad too.

Our time together as one was short and too quickly everything went back as it was.

Once I sat, with tears still streaming and an occasional whimper, everyone looked. They said nothing but must have known I'd had a very emotional experience.

As I looked at everyone, I noticed Crystal was no longer with us.

Phreya

Once Mrs Osbourne had finished talking about the other four and her demonstrations, I answered her question, then she came to me. The fact she was my teacher and none of the others knew her, I was a little disappointed she didn't discuss me first.

"Can anyone tell me anything about beliefs?" she asked.

Immediately I said, "They aren't always true."

"And why is that?"

"Because I believe I'm supposed to be a boy and I'm not."

She said, "Belief is what makes your perception of the world exactly what it is. They are just thoughts you keep thinking, and as you continue and share them, some will also come to believe them too and so on until the point is reached when it becomes the same for the majority.

"You are a boy here with us today, and on your planet, they perform procedures to make people look different to what they currently are. So, nothing is really as it seems. The reason things don't happen the way people want is because they don't believe. Have you heard that your world used to be flat?"

We all laughed and said, "Yes."

"This may amuse you, but the reason this was so was because people couldn't comprehend stability on a spherical planet. Flat was all they understood.

"In their old way of thinking, they believed anything placed on a rotating sphere would fall off, and your laws of physics state this. So, in their minds, there was no way possible for Earth to be anything but flat and there was little to convince them otherwise.

"But let me assure you today, all ways of thinking become old eventually, and with new thinking comes change. Sometimes for the better, sometimes not, but either way, it comes. So, no matter what you want from your lives, belief is the key to it all!"

That hit me to the core.

I was happy the lesson was almost over because I could think of nothing else.

Lastly, she said, "Before we finish, is there anything you would like to ask us?"

Crystal

As everyone's apparition opened the last part of the lesson for questions, being everything in the moment, I became everyone's apparition and I was the one giving the final part of the lesson.

Claudia was the first to ask as she was thinking of saving her mother from her accident in the aircraft. "As well as different dimensions or realities, do we time travel too?"

This was a question I was interested in knowing too. I didn't know the answer personally, but it flowed through me for the benefit of everyone.

"Everything in your life, without exception, is subject to your perception. The point at which you leave the reality you are in causes that timeline to become potential once again. However, as you leave, the trace elements of gold within you are drawn out by your ball and anchored there. So, every time you journey, the ball will always follow them back to the source.

"No matter how long you think you are away, they always get you back home, and you will always return at the exact point you left. It may appear dream-like, but there is no time lapse and the difference is you remember everything about it. These memories do not fade like dreams.

"As for time travel as a physical being, there is no such thing. So, make no mistake about this. It may appear that you travel through time or end up in times past, but what you are actually doing is inter-dimensional travel through potential.

"For any physical being, time only goes forwards. However, you can arrive at a place which seems to be past, but it will be in an alternate reality, a potential reality that could have been.

"The only form of time travel available to any physical being is that of memory, which can be relived as many times as desired. You may remember them differently from time to time, but the original experience of that which has been lived by you does not change."

The knowledge was flowing through me and I was absorbing it as I passed it on. Some of the people with us at that time, especially Claudia, seemed to be a little disappointed by this but the questions continued.

Artemis asked, "Do timelines ever cross or blend together?"

"Without the crossing of timelines, you would not be. It happens constantly and it isn't just a few. It is many potentials crossing and creating one conceivable reality. When this happens, you are tuning in and this is where your thoughts emerge.

"The more potentials that cross give different outcomes. After thoughts come actions, then manifestation. Times when thoughts come and no action is taken, more potentials are attracted.

"We know actions have to be taken so we arrange for the potentials to cross, and those are the times when you can't not do something. So, it is the potential from converging realities that bring manifestation into your reality."

Annie raised her hand and asked, "All the abilities we have, can we use them whenever we want?"

"You can use them when the time is right, and the time will be right when they are needed. It will take you a while to learn a process and use them in your true reality. But, when that time comes, you cannot use them just to show people your ability. That's not why you have them.

"When you travel as a group, all powers and abilities will have the opportunity to manifest. Once you have mastered your own abilities, the opportunity to create new ones will arise.

"And on the subject of abilities, you all have your Brumalis to help you travel and soon you will each receive a ring with a unique stone. This will help you with the different powers. Some of which you are yet to acquire.

Initially, these items are essential as your belief will be in them rather than in yourselves. They will help strengthen your beliefs in your abilities, but in time you will realise they aren't necessary. This is why humanity has lucky charms."

As this information was sinking in, an urge came over me to ask the students a question.

"We are surprised no one has asked about the numbers as we have consistently presented them to you. Araminter, do you know what they are?"

Surprised that we came to her so unexpectedly, she automatically said, "No."

"Think again."

Sat quietly for a while, she said, "Sixteen and eighteen."

"Life is a mathematical manifestation. The golden ratio, 1.618 or Phi, is the basis of creation as you know it. Ever present throughout the universe, seen and unseen, and as with the crossing of timelines, without it you would not be."

On sharing this, I felt the revelation Araminter experienced. She realised it wasn't a meeting at the Golden R at 10. It was the golden ratio. It was creation.

"Also, there is 1111, a superstition created by humanity. This is the sign of new beginnings. The meaning of these two numbers together is why you manifested on this plane. You will be the cause of humanity's new beginning, bringing a new perception and a future of joy to their existence, which will emanate throughout the universe, benefitting all consciousness."

The sharing of this information was the beginning of deep contemplation, no questions were being thought of, only solutions to what we suspected humanity's plight was.

I could feel there was much more wanting to be asked, but most were still processing all that had been shared. No one raised their hand or offered a vibration, so I continued to end the lesson.

On completion, each planetary race grouped together to discuss their learning. I joined our group as our surroundings disappeared. We were now in an oasis with sand as far as the eye could see.

Discussing our lesson, Arty blurted out, "All seeing! Glass ears!"

We all looked at her. Everyone in earshot looked at her.

We laughed at first at the random nonsensical outburst, but then I noticed a haze was interfering with the colour of their thoughts and their colours began to dull.

A warning sign.

The majority of our knowledge was intuitive, but without fail it was correct every time.

As this thought shared itself amongst the group, a solitary marble with an encased ear rolled past us and stopped. Turning and stopping with speed, looking and listening. Absorbing information from its surroundings.

Claudia

Earlier, when the light beams penetrated our foreheads, I felt Amelia's anguish for Phreya and I knew immediately what was required of me.

His feelings for Crystal were personal and though the others knew there was something not right with him, we knew what it was. This inner conflict began with his first sight of her.

Artemis' outburst interrupted my thoughts and although we laughed, we were surprised to see an ear encapsulated within a glass ball, but considering all we'd encountered, it wasn't that strange. We'd encountered far stranger things on our journeys, and never knowing where we would end up, this time was no different. We had no idea where in the universe we were, and everyone present felt the ripple.

The oasis became silent, then discussions of what this irregularity meant ensued. This was our first encounter of this anomaly. How it felt to us was like the force, the one that had exploded around us at our first union, was returning to its source.

We didn't know why, but this caused an atmosphere amongst those present. It was palpable and in quick succession, each planetary race departed.

Artemis had followed the marble and was nowhere to be seen and with everyone else gone, we were the only ones left.

With only six of us now present, our combined power was reduced seven-fold and as the teaching energies had departed on termination of the lesson, we were alone.

With everyone else deep in discussion of what to do about Arty, I went to meditate alone.

With a clear mind, I focused on Phreya's earlier embarrassment wondering what I could create to help him keep his private thoughts private.

Devoid of reality of any kind, the clarity in the depths of my mind was pristine. Sat silently ignoring the conversations from the others, I had the overwhelming feeling of being suppressed. Then, within the emptiness, I was being shown a ring, circled by six letters.

PHREZA.

I wondered for a moment why Phreya's name was spelt incorrectly, then I verbalised it.

Frazer.

I liked the sound of that. I thought this might be the name he should be known as when he was a boy.

Not knowing how to manifest such a creation, I didn't even try. If this was for him, it would manifest somehow.

I was brought out of my meditative state by a much stronger ripple and a sudden silence. The other five had stopped talking.

I opened my eyes to see Phreya sat on the floor with his head in his hands and the others looking up at something hovering just out of their reach above their heads.

As I got closer, I realised it was the ring. I asked where it came from and was told Araminter's pocket.

In our lesson, Pneuma told us she was the Manifester, so I assumed she created it from Phreya's desire, but it must have already been there because she said she'd forgotten about it.

On recognition, I told them it was for Phreya.

They all looked at me then at Phreya. He stood and looked at it as it began to descend. While I told him what it was for, he took it and put it onto his finger. The relief on his face was evident

I told them we would eventually have one each, but what they would be for, I didn't know.

What started as a vibration in Araminter's pocket was to be Phreya's ring of concealment which not only kept his thoughts private but ours too.

As long as we were with him.

The marble returned and was circling us, but Artemis was nowhere to be seen.

Antonis

Still no closer to his goal, he was thinking of the many uneventful years since the storm. With classical music playing quietly in the background, he hadn't noticed the marble raise from the desk and begin to spin. Deep in contemplation, his peace was broken by the ripple.

The most recent had been caused by him, so to experience one without prior knowledge was more than unexpected.

He leapt from his chair and ran to the door. He opened it and peered along the corridor.

Stood outside her office, Uma was talking to Colin. She turned to see him with a look of great concern on his face. She asked if everything was all right but without response, he turned and slammed the door.

Walking towards his desk, he noticed it. From mid-air, he snatched the marble and held it against his ear. Listening and feeling intently, he interpreted the vibrations.

With the blinds either side of his door always closed, he locked the door.

Lost on his own path, he still spoke his daily chants, but with the millennia of life experienced, he modified them to benefit his cause.

Sat in his chair, he moved forwards and reached for his Radley handbag. Placed centrally in front of him, he removed the tag and charm from the loop at the side of the handle. He tied it to the centre of the arched handle and folded it towards him to suspend the charm.

With both hands now on his desk, one palm facing down and the other in a fist facing upwards holding the marble tight, he chanted.

"Om mani padme hum. Mandala mantara auralocular. Prakat karana."

As he repeated this, his eye began to weep a white fluid. He took the first white tear and rubbed it on the bag charm. The white fluid continued to stream until his eyeball became transparent, then a black fluid followed. The lack of melanin in his eyes left a green pigment floating in the transparency.

He raised his fist and forced the marble into the socket causing blood to squirt and seep through his fingers. Now in the socket, but bulging, he began to shake violently whilst shouting, "one, one, one one." He did this constantly until the shaking stopped.

He heard a knock on the door, followed by Uma's voice. He saw the handle being moved up and down and was glad he had locked the room from the inside.

With long deep breaths and cupped hands below the dog charm, it changed. The majority of the gold from it began to vaporise and form a wispy thread making its way to the marble in Ant's eye socket and, in the process, revealing a fully grown white Scottie dog attached to the bag handle. The remaining gold was around its neck. The golden lead and collar were his connection and his way back.

With his last deep breath, he exhaled it gently in the direction of the dog and breathed life into it. Tongue hanging out, it sat staring and panting as if it was waiting for something.

Ant began to chant again.

"Fulminare, fulminare, fulminare. Om mani padme hum. Vi veri universum vivus vici. Semper invicta. Revelare lux brumalis. Victoria aut mors."

Ant heard shuffling outside his office. His colleagues were obviously eavesdropping on his activities. The door flew off its hinges towards him. Everything around him did the same.

The universe was collapsing towards the bag.

Uma and Colin were desperately holding onto the door frame as the attraction to the bag lifted them off their feet. Horizontal and slowly losing their grip, the attraction was too strong.

Once they were in the bag, everything around Ant changed from physical form to multi-coloured light and from all directions, the universe was being sucked into the handbag's vortex.

Ant stood; the desk and chair were the last things he saw enter the bag.

The dog and the bag fell to the floor and as Ant turned to the light and disappeared into the bag, the vortex diminished and the bag closed.

The surrounding light folded up around the dog. The bag formed a ball then shrunk to become a point of light.

Artemis

Though it's against our culture to take something from the land, I wasn't sure if this fell into that category. I was intrigued by the marble and I wanted it, so I decided to follow it, but as hard as I tried, I couldn't get close enough to catch it. It was like a cat that didn't want to be picked up.

I had been following it for a while when it stopped and began to head in my direction. I thought it was coming to me, so I squatted down with both hands in front. Just as it was about to roll into my hands, it launched itself over my head and shot off with such speed, I couldn't be bothered to chase it.

All alone with no idea where the others were or how to get back to them, I sat for a while. I could have called them all to me but I didn't want to interrupt whatever it was they may have been doing.

As I sat alone, thinking of Gambu and the lesson, there was another ripple, along with the feeling of an increase in pressure. This one felt like what I imagine an earthquake to be.

I looked around and, in the distance, boab trees appeared. The familiarity comforted me so I headed towards them. I hoped it would be similar to my place. I could have done with a swim.

Annie

I didn't say much during the discussion of the lesson or about the ripple, but just prior to the second stronger ripple and descending pressure, the marble returned and began to encircle us.

The moles on the side of my head began to pulse. I put my finger on them to find out if there was a message or if it was pulsing as a warning of something. I felt the raised bumps and it spelt: Leave now.

Thanks to Phreya's ring, the message was concealed and only I knew of it, but I knew we had to follow this instruction, so I released it for the rest of the group. They immediately stopped talking and looked at me.

The pit of my stomach was doing somersaults. As my senses are more acute than the others, I could smell the overwhelming scent of a dog and in the distance, I heard a rumble.

We all felt the urgency of the situation and knew we had to start our balls quickly, but with Artemis gone, doing it with a lace was going to take far longer.

Phreya was the only one wearing footwear with laces and I was hoping the aglet was thin enough to fit the holes in each ball.

The rumble was getting closer and I could now feel the low vibration of it.

I was beginning to panic. I knew we had to leave now, but Phreya was taking too long.

Long laces bowed and knotted were pulled too tight and he was having trouble undoing them. We needed both so we could start two balls at a time

The panic that began with me was spreading through the group and now, they could hear and feel the rumble.

With one lace out and Crystal's Brumalis started, our anxiety was still growing.

Phreya suggested each person should leave once theirs had been started, but Crystal thought about the last two, wondering what would happen if one didn't start or reach speed in time.

Not knowing what fate awaited us, she thought we would be better off together.

Artemis

The boab trees were unusual here. They looked as if they'd been crossed with the jacaranda. The beautiful purple blue canopy threw shade all along my path as I walked towards the brow of a hill. Reaching the top and looking into the distance, I saw my path had many forks, but each one led to the same place. I raised my gaze to behold a village of opal. The sheer beauty of it attracted me.

Getting closer, I noticed there was a group of people. They looked as if they were waiting for something. As I reached them, I recognised them as elders that had passed from my world, stood as if to welcome me. They weren't looking in my direction but at a large clock hanging from a ghost gum tree.

In unison, they began to speak. At first, I thought they were going to perform a Welcome to Country, but in our tribe's language they repeated, "Look at the clock, it's time."

I looked up to see the large opal dial edged with gold. With no numbers, the FRAZER branded clock had three hands. They moved to create an inverted star and the time it told was "Now", "Now" and "Present".

The vivid colours of the opal and the name reminded me of Phreya. Something began to bother me about Phreya but I couldn't recall what it was. I thought Frazer would be a good boy's name for him. That thought brought another and I wondered what they were doing.

I should have called them to me then, but I was so intrigued with the opaline village, I wanted to explore for a while first.

I was about to ask the elders about the village but as I looked to where they were stood, there was no sign of them.

I walked through the deserted village. The houses looked very small, so I went to look inside one. I went up the steps and on reaching the top, the door opened automatically.

It was not what I expected to see.

I thought, *How can such a small building house the palace that surrounds me? This house must have come from the minds of gods.*

Marble floors and pillars, opal walls, and windows of every precious and semi-precious transparent stone, tinting the shards of light as they passed through onto the iridescent colours of the opal. But the rooms were empty.

I found that very odd.

I wondered about bedrooms. How would anyone sleep here? Miraculously, beds appeared.

Amazed by this, I thought, *what about a kitchen?* The beds were replaced with a stove, a refrigerator, a dining table and chairs.

Then I thought about what Gambu told me about having a clear mind. That was important here as my thoughts were manifesting immediately.

Claudia

While waiting for Phreya, the rhythmic rumble came through the air as well as the ground and from one direction only.

I turned to see in the distance a small figure making slow steady steps towards us. Every step stirred the sand and even from where I was stood, I could see the breath of this being move the dust from his line of sight. The pulsing rhythmic rumble was in time with his breathing, which had the intensity and roughness of a roar.

Worry began to set in as Phreya had only one lace out. I was beginning to understand how Amelia felt when she had the urge to help others and keep them safe.

There was now an urgency to our plight. This being was slowly gaining ground and with no idea of its intention, departure was our only option.

Phreya finally had the other lace free. I took it from him and nervously fumbling, I eventually got the lace in and wound it onto his Brumalis. With a quick pull, it started.

Amelia had already started Crystal's and she was stood looking towards the gaining being. As it was getting closer, I noticed a gold light emerge from Crystal's chest increasing with every step the being made.

Eventually, it encased the whole of her. The light emanating from her lit the land as bright as the sun and in addition to the daylight, we could see further than normal. Her light picked out everything.

I took Amelia's hand and inserted the lace and started her Brumalis.

"Oh no," she said.

I looked at her and she had a look of horror on her face.

"What's wrong?" I asked.

She pointed to the figure approaching us.

I didn't see it at first, but the longer I stared and the closer he got, he looked like Ian M. Bude, the security guard that handcuffed us. He was carrying something in his left hand.

As we realised this, so did the other four.

With four balls started, we stopped and stared in the direction of the assumed threat.

When they all saw him for themselves, we were about to start the remaining balls when a figure from behind him appeared. It took a wide path around and headed behind us.

Now with two adversaries, our time was running out.

Amelia

Seeing the shop security guard again only added to my panic and now he had an ally. It looked like there was no way out of this for us.

Filled with dread, we'd forgotten what we were taught shortly before about Araminter's manifesting abilities and our safe haven that would protect us and allow us to rest. We were all focused on getting the balls started and getting out of this place.

I took Araminter's hand, inserted the lace into hers and started it. With only Annie's and Claudia's to start, we were almost ready to spin in unison.

Claudia started Annie's ball, then I started hers.

By the time all balls were started, Crystal had disappeared within her glow, and although we knew she was there, we couldn't see her. Just a golden globe.

We looked just in front of her and there he was. A tall Mediterranean-looking man. He looked like the people we saw on the street when Claudia and I were taken on our first encounter.

With a close-cut manicured beard and moustache, dressed in a royal blue pinstripe suit and tan brogues, he was carrying a handbag. Though it wasn't physical, in Crystal's glow its multiple colours shimmered with the iridescence of Phreya's ring. He looked very respectable and under normal circumstances, not scary at all, but his presence was threatening.

Then he spoke.

I wasn't sure whether or not he knew there were five others behind Crystal and still peering around, I saw a bolt of light shoot from her orb and hit the man square in the chest. A voice followed.

Crystal

The marble was still circling us, spiralling from the ground to above our heads with such speed we dared not attempt to move outside of it for fear of being struck.

Staring into the distance, he came into view wearing something like a cowboy hat, only not. The closer he came, the stronger the feeling in my chest became and as before, I was becoming a channel for the eternal ephemeral energies, observing the actions of the approaching figure.

The previous panic dissipated and I was at peace. Innately I knew no harm would come to us, but still scared because I didn't know how or why.

Phreya and the girls were behind me frantically trying to start everyone's ball and stalling this man was buying us time to facilitate our escape.

Even though his presentation wasn't intimidating, I knew there was imminent danger for us and I was waiting for some kind of action from him.

He stood directly in front of me and as he raised his left hand, he caught the speeding marble. After wiping it in the handkerchief from his top pocket, he proceeded to force it into his right eye socket. The blood and other fluid that squirted from the applied pressure landed at his feet.

From there, it crept slowly towards me like pumping veins. I felt as if a connection was wanting to be made but they couldn't penetrate my light.

Unable to connect, they continued around me and circled the others, spitting out thorns in their wake.

He spoke with a soft endearing voice. I felt he was yearning for something.

"I never expected my quest to be so difficult. I have been searching for millennia through many dimensions and realities for your light. I have completed most of what I believe was required of me. The final step being our union.

"You are the light of winter. You have been absent from the world for too long and though I have tried, humanity's wellbeing is spiralling out of control. Together, we can bring about a new beginning and end the suffering through the light we will share."

As he delivered his monologue, I felt myself losing control of my body and ability to respond. I became the observer.

He chanted, "Om mani padme hum," and opened his arms as if to receive something from the light of my glow.

The channelled energies responded.

"Antonis Backlav, you were one of the great students of our message, but as you have navigated your path, you forgot the essence of it, and you are no longer pure of heart. We have observed your actions over millennia and to our disbelief, your life search of finding peace amongst nations has turned you into the oppressor you are attempting to banish. As a result of this, you are now the one to be banished and not by us, but by your own hand."

Phreya

With all Brumalis spinning, we were focused and ready to leap. The atmosphere was tense as we listened to the man speak and the response from Crystal. When we heard her say he was the one to be banished, we braced ourselves.

For him, this was an unwanted revelation. For us, we knew no good could come of it.

No sooner had the words left Crystal, her golden orb flickered. It shot a bolt far into the distance on my left then disappeared for a while. When it disappeared, we heard a single bark of a dog.

Before her light returned, we could see past her. The man in the suit lay stunned on the ground; his hat still in the air falling to the ground and a handbag near to his side. The look on his face was one of shock. He wasn't expecting to see more than one person. This enraged him and, after raising himself from the ground, he charged towards us.

Crystal joined us and completed our circle. We began to spin our balls faster in an attempt to leave this place, but instead of entering a statically charged tunnel, we became encased within a ball of white light. It was like a forcefield of light protecting us.

The rage in his face didn't match his manner. He calmly said, "Your light is split and not fully present. The strength of power you command is lacking and of no match to that which I am. Your light may protect you, but that too will pass."

He held out both arms and commanded the surrounding veins and thorns. They rose from the ground, attached themselves and grew around the ball of light like a cage. The thorns pierced the light and exposed eyeballs on their ends, and we all had the feeling they were absorbing something from each of us.

The girth of the thorns grew, causing fractures in the light and we were now worried he would eventually be able to reach us, but the larger the fractures became, the more clearly we were able to see him.

It seemed he had a better view of us too, but as we looked closer into his vibrant green eyes, we saw he was looking behind us.

So focused on the man, we'd forgotten his ally was behind us.

I turned to see the pale blue uniformed figure staring through the thorny, vein-encased light at the man.

I recognised her at once. It was the woman with the dark glasses from the store but she was wearing a hospital porter's uniform. Once I recognised her, the adornments I knew disappeared to reveal an angelic aura.

When they made eye contact, there was another look of shock on his face. On recognition, he attempted to run directly through the light towards his supposed ally but was propelled away by the power protecting us.

His ally walked around us to face him and spoke before calmly entering our light.

Today wasn't a good day for Antonis.

Araminter

As with all my travels, the effect of my extra chromosome was intermittent. I used to be envious of others and wanted to be like them, but once I had experienced life as they did, I realised I preferred life with it.

To be the same was novel at first, and it had some benefits, like the situation we were currently in, but overall, my life was far better with 47.

I suppose I had the best of both worlds. Whenever there was an urgency, it would be absent and these were the times when my understanding and comprehension was quick.

The urgency of our situation now needed to be addressed. We were all now frantically spinning, trying to reach revolutionary speed when an angelic being entered our sphere. Though our situation scared us, we felt we knew her. Her calming presence focused us.

She told us to breathe. Slowly and with intent.

I was trying to focus on Artemis. We were all concerned for her, not knowing whether or not this man had already seen her, and if so, had he harmed her?

Occasionally opening my eyes, I saw the man continually circling the light, staring at each one of us as he passed. By the way he looked at us, I could tell he was memorising every aspect. Height, shape, age, hair, eyes, everything. He was very intimidating.

His eyes were of the deepest green and glowing bright as he spoke in an almost possessed way.

Artemis

I left the house with some despair. It was beautiful inside but the speedy manifestation of thought scared me. I needed to be with the others.

I started my ball, sat quietly and closed my eyes.

Calming the chatter of my mind, I focused on the others. Individually at first, then as a group. I began with Amelia through to Crystal. Thinking of the speed at which they appeared the last time comforted me, and if everything manifested immediately in this place, then they would be here as soon as I was focused.

But it was taking too long, nothing was happening.

I did the same again and still nothing. Something was wrong.

I opened my eyes to see a golden bolt of charged light heading towards me. I tried to move away from its path but it hit my hand directly. The charge from the light was what I would imagine an electric shock to be like. It was lucky I was seated because every muscle in my body tensed.

My mind went blank and I was unable to form a single thought, but when it stopped, I was left with an image of a man. I had seen him before.

He was the man wearing the Akubra at the billabong.

Unsure of whether the electrical discharge had affected my ball, I tried to start it again. Thankfully, the force was almost immediate.

Trying to keep this image from my mind, I meditated a while before attempting to call them to me again.

During meditation and prior to their arrival, I encountered an angelic being, though it was clearly a woman's form, her energy was both masculine and feminine. She sat facing me. Taking both my hands, she looked through my eyes and deep inside.

"Artemis, you have the most powerful of the quasars and that is key to the group, so if you continue along a path of personal exploration in other dimensions, the safety of your friends will be in jeopardy.

"The worlds you experience are always there for you, so there is no urgency or need to wander alone and to be with just one other will always be of great benefit to yourself and them."

Her energies came through as she spoke. The conviction in her voice was very masculine but her delivery was femininely gentle. It reminded me of Phreya.

Sophia

The implosion of the universe disturbed all energies.

I knew this was the doing of Antonis Backlav. A great student he was until he lost his path. It was widely believed it was my passing that changed him. My physical death made him view the world in a different light and from that day, he saw very little good in people and from his subsequent life experiences, he adopted a very different direction to that which he was studying. The complete opposite to the one he was currently treading.

Connected across realms, he was unable to accept the message I constantly presented and he became lost in his own world. He was a master of the universe but because of the path he chose, he lost his affinity with good and the choices he made reflected that.

He had been on his quest for omnipotence for millennia, and now he was the closest he'd ever been.

We could not let this come to pass.

Focused on the oasis ahead of him, he was oblivious to anything else around him. I followed as he stirred up sand ahead of him and left a sandstorm in his wake. Unable to see what it was within the oasis he was so focused on, I took a wide berth.

Still unseen, the golden orb came into view.

Focused on Antonis and the orb, I made my way to the back of it, so as not to alert him to my presence.

I watched and listened to his words as he approached the light encasing the children and it was when he finished speaking that he noticed me.

It had been over two thousand years since we were together and though he cloaked it well, I could still feel his vulnerability.

Beneath his immaculately dressed bravado was the lost boy I knew so long ago. All he had endured hadn't led him where his path was meant to.

We made eye contact.

He sped towards the fragmented light sphere heading straight for me, but the light wasn't broken yet or fractured enough for him to pass through. It expelled him back into the sand.

I walked through the light and knelt by his side.

In his presence, I felt almost human again. A strange sensation but to be physical again was not something I desired. Free and limitless was how I currently intended to spend my eternity.

I explained the afterlife to him and asked him to give up his quest and come with me and we could do good together from the ethers.

Even though his eyes were deep green with remnants of envy, I still felt his love for me. But he grew angry and pushed me away.

Antonis

The information the marble absorbed caused it to swell to double its normal size and with no time to chant, the fluid in his eyeball was still present. The insertion into his eye socket was brutal.

Being a part of him, the fluid was connected and he orchestrated it like a master conductor to form a cage around the light trapping the occupants within.

With his two marble eyes, he could see the sphere, and with the thorn eyes that pierced the light, he had a 360-degree view within.

He was a worldly man with knowledge of all races and knew immediately these were all aboriginal children.

His eyes absorbed every detail of Phreya and the girls. Five girls, one long haired boy, two of the girls bald. With her golden orb intact, Crystal wasn't visible to him but when her light flickered previously, her image ingrained itself in his memory: a purple haired aboriginal girl.

Defeat was not in his remit and he would never give up any quest. They were always seen through to the very end. It was always victory or death for him and so far, he had been victorious.

He believed he had all the necessary information about the bearers of the winter light and should he not succeed at this time, he knew Australia was where his search in the real world would begin.

He approached the sphere and spoke, telling of their splintered light, but when he finished, he saw through the light and recognised his long dead wife.

Attempting to run through the light, he was violently expelled by its force. On his back in the sand, he saw her walking towards him. She lifted his head in her hand and kissed his forehead.

"My dearest Antonis, how I've longed for this moment to be with you once again. I so wanted to incarnate again just to be in your presence, but you changed so quickly.

"So bright and intuitive, you were the beacon humanity needed. You do not have to continue on this path. You can come with me and we can continue this together without limits and with no harm to anyone."

He listened to what she had to say but couldn't help the feeling of being betrayed by his wife.

He knew she sensed this. She kissed him once again, said farewell and walked into the light.

Antonis got to his feet, collected his hat and bag and walked in her wake. Still unable to penetrate the light, he looked within and in a booming voice said, "I am Ant Backlav. I am VANTABLACK. I have been inside the mind of two and now your union is complete, I know your essence.

"I entered your minds in my realm, but I live in yours. The coming was only meant to be one but you are the manifestation of the fractured light of winter, and I now have to make the six whole again. So, I will say this only once. Give me the quasars or join me!"

The children were silent and looking to Sophia for guidance. But she offered none.

This was a collective choice they had to make alone.

With no action from them, Antonis continued. "Being unyielding, you have now put your people at risk and there will be much death and destruction for the custodians of your land unless you relinquish that which I desire. The fractures within your protective light are growing large, and you know once I enter, I will take them from you, and Sophia can't protect you from me so make your decision."

The thoughts they shared were unanimous. Ant heard the choice they made.

We can't give this power to such a man.

Sophia smiled.

Annie

I thought back to our adventure in Virtue. Was he the source of the uneasiness I felt when I had perfect sight?

I said to the group we should open our channels of thought so Artemis would know what's happening and she could call us to her if we were unable to leave.

The urgency of our situation had us shaking with fear. Too focused to cry, we put an arm on each other's shoulder to form a circle and sent our thoughts to Artemis. I felt she wasn't too far away.

Our channels opened and a wisp of light from each of our spinning Brumalis entered our throat chakras, exited from the third eye chakra and merged at the centre of our circle. It continued vertical then veered off in the direction of the bolt that left Crystal's orb earlier.

Being the focus of our thought, I believed this light was heading to Artemis.

The cracks in the light surrounding us were now almost large enough for this man to squeeze through. We were worried but he just stood there, calmly waiting until he could stroll through without effort.

We had been spinning for some time now and my arm was getting weak. I thought if we didn't leap soon, we would be done for.

I turned to look at Sophia. She smiled then disappeared.

The light surrounding us grew stronger, gradually sealing the cracks and becoming whole once more. Safe within the light, we stopped spinning our balls and though we couldn't see outside of it, we began to move.

The silence was broken by his booming voice as he shouted, "Fulminare!"

On the outer surface of our encasement, we saw the lightning strike and the single bark we heard earlier was now constant.

Silence again.

The constant pressure we felt prior to Ant's arrival had now lifted, and we didn't know if it was that or because our ordeal was over but we felt lighter, like we had been unburdened.

We heard Artemis' voice. "Are you in there?"

"We are but we don't know how to stop the light," Phreya replied. "It's coming from all the Brumalis. They're still spinning and we don't know how to stop them."

Artemis was silent for a while then said, "Let's meditate together, clear our minds and let the universe do what it does."

We sat in silence with our eyes closed, hoping we could escape our protective orb.

Antonis

Lightning bolts began to shoot from the point of light.

Being the last to enter the bag, he was the first out. The point of light grew large and, from within, he became physical once more.

After his manifestation, he calmed the dog who was growling and shaking the bag violently from side to side by its handles, spewing the universe from within. The dog returned to become the bag charm again.

Ant sat at his desk to see Colin and Uma being propelled through the doorway followed by the office door which reattached perfectly to the hinges and remained locked.

He heard someone talking outside the door. He looked up to see Colin barge through, taking it back off its hinges.

"What the hell is going on?" Ant asked.

Colin looked embarrassed and stumbled over his words as if he didn't know what to say. Which was just as well.

Ant ordered him out and told Uma to follow.

As soon as they left and were in their own offices, he took a piece of Meteorological Service of Canada headed paper and proceeded to pen his resignation.

On completion, he picked up the phone and booked a first-class ticket to Perth.

Western Australia.

Poem

SHE

Society breached an obligation to she
he, never questioned why.
The powers granted were taken so but,
never did she cry.

A right from birth so he believed
always taught 'be strong',
the shadows held the meeker sex
yet, she knew all along

the true power they held within,
let he believe was his,
to make a world of love and peace but,
that's not what it is.

This power, their jewel they hold within
too precious to use in vain,
compassionate, caring, exuding love,
why can't he think the same.

The time arrived for she to shine and,
put right all the wrong,
with love for he, she takes his hand and,
in her heart, with song.

Shadows break and strength appears,
society is shaken.
Divine is she, remembering
all that's been forsaken.

In retrospect he pondered life,
morally in arrears.
How wrong he was, unaware
the decision always hers.
So look inside, deep within
eventually you'll find
that little girl you thought you'd lost.

The she that makes you shine.